THE
MELANCHOLY OF
MECHAGIRL

CATHERYNNE M. VALENTE

HAIKA
SORU

THE
MELANCHOLY OF
MECHAGIRL

STORIES AND POEMS

BY
CATHERYNNE M. VALENTE

SAN FRANCISCO

THE MELANCHOLY OF MECHAGIRL
©2013 Catherynne M. Valente

See Publication History for individual story and poem publications.

Cover art by Yuko Shimizu
Design by Fawn Lau
All rights reserved.

HAIKASORU
Published by VIZ Media, LLC
PO Box 77010
San Francisco, CA 94107

www.haikasoru.com

Library of Congress Cataloging-in-Publication Data

Valente, Catherynne M., 1979–
  [Works. Selections]
  The melancholy of mechagirl : stories and poems / Catherynne Valente.
      pages cm
  ISBN 978-1-4215-5613-0
  I. Title.
  PS3622.A4258A6 2013
  813'.6--dc23

                                                2013015259

Printed in the U.S.A.
First printing, July 2013

CONTENTS

INTRODUCTION

BY TERUYUKI HASHIMOTO

This is Catherynne M. Valente's collection of the stories and poems with a connection to Japan. In the stories with less of a connection, the references to Japan are subtle and as hard to distinguish as a thread woven into fabric. You will also notice other recurring themes. Descriptions of houses and families appear several times. A wife is separated from her husband, and disparate people (and non-human beings) find themselves sharing the same house. The stories are all dressed differently and are quite original. But if you have encountered this author's works before, you already know how the worlds she depicts are unfamiliar, and you can continue without any trouble and never lose the way. Her prose is as carefully refined as a smoothly paved road.

I first came across Valente's work in 2010 when her novel *Palimpsest* was nominated for the Hugo Award for Best Novel. I visited her website and found that some of her works were influenced by Japanese culture. For example, the title of one of her books, *Yume No Hon: The Book of Dreams* (2005), is in Japanese, and she named her monthly letter project after *omikuji*, fortunes written on paper strips and sold in shrines and temples. Soon after I started reading her stories, I realized that her interest in Japan is informed by both study and by authentic lived experience.

Did you know that there are 45,000 US soldiers living in Japan? There are another 45,000 members of military families here as well. Valente spent several years living in Japan as part of a Navy family. Consequently, some of her stories seem semiautobiographical, such as "Fifteen Panels Depicting the Sadness of the Baku and the Jotai," and "Ink, Water, Milk," the latter of which was written for this collection. Both stories are set in Yokosuka, a city with a US Navy base, and in both appear *yokai*, imaginary creatures, and a lonely Navy wife.

Japanese mythology is a hybrid of indigenous folklore and *Shinto* religion, Buddhism, and foreign myths and folklore, which came to Japan from Eurasia via China. By paging through just the beginning of this book, you will come across the said "Fifteen Panels Depicting the Sadness of the Baku and the Jotai," on the chaos of Yokosuka—and Paradise—described in a manner that will totally blow you away. In this powerful opening story, Valente introduces her Japanesque view of the world and quickly immerses you in it.

You will see many yokai in this book. *Yokai* are imaginary Japanese creatures such as fairies, ghosts, and monsters from myths and folktales. During the Edo period, book-rental shops became common, and leisure reading became a popular hobby in Japanese cities. In those days, yokai were an especially popular theme, and many *ukiyo-e* artists drew yokai pictures. One of these artists, Toriyama Sekien (1712–1788), made some yokai picture books. He drew famous traditional yokai as well as some he created himself. *Kyorinrin* and *Futsukeshibaba*, which appear in "Ink, Water, Milk," are understood to be Sekien's creations.

Valente finds inspiration in traditional yokai tales but doesn't simply retell classic stories. In "One Breath, One Stroke," she describes Sazae-Oni (the Horned Turban shell spirit or Snail Woman), a Japanese version of a Siren, in this way: "Sazae-Onna lives in a pond in the floor of the kitchen. Her shell is tiered like a cake or a palace, hard and thorned and colored like the inside of an almond, with seams of mother of pearl swirling in spiral patterns over her gnarled surface. She eats the rice that falls from the table when the others sit down to supper. She drinks the steam from the teakettle." Valente here shows us her version of cute Sazae-Oni that no one else would ever imagine.

The image of Japan in Anglophone science fiction has tended to take the form of futuristic megacities, such as Chiba City in *Neuromancer* by William Gibson. This trend continues today. New writers such as Lauren Beukes and Hannu Rajaniemi have described imaginary future Tokyos—and their work is funny and good—but megacities represent only a small facet of Japan. This country is long, spanning from north to south, and it has many suburban areas, rural locations, and historical ruins. Valente has written about places in Japan not widely portrayed in science fiction and fantasy before, for example, Hokkaido, the northernmost prefecture on the Russian border. She also explores Hashima, a small uninhabited island known as Gunkanjima, where over five thousand people once worked in a coal mine, in "Ghosts of Gunkanjima."

In reading this collection, you may discover not only another view of Japan, but also another side of the author, thanks to the stories she published in *Clarkesworld Magazine*. These include "Silently and Very Fast," which according to Valente is "real science fiction." This family history story begins in the near cyberpunkish future and ends in the age of Singularity. It is rich in references to myths and folktales as well. "Thirteen Ways of Looking at Space/Time" is also an ambitious story. It dismantles and reconstructs Creation myths from around the world in scientific terms. "Fade to White" is a dystopian story set in the days after the apocalypse with a slight fragrance of Japanese history. Valente is a masterful "story engineer," one who adapts and transforms traditional terms and symbols to tell thoroughly modern stories. She demonstrates her power in a freer and more dynamic way in these new pieces. Through the latest work, I am certain that Valente should, and likely will, continue transforming and soaring far beyond possible boundaries of country, new and old, genre and everything.

Imagine this book as a set of traditional Japanese paper doors. By turning the pages, you slide the doors open. Soon you will enter a place where you have never been.

Teruyuki Hashimoto is a Japanese reviewer and critic of science fiction, mainly for Hayakawa's *SF Magazine*. Born in Hokkaido in 1984, Hashimoto currently lives in Tokyo.

THE MELANCHOLY OF MECHAGIRL

X Prefecture drive time radio
 trills and pops
its pink rhinestone bubble tunes—
pipe that sound into my copper-riveted heart,
that softgirl/brightgirl/candygirl electrocheer gigglenoise
right down through the steelfrown tunnels of my
all-hearing head.
 Best stay
out of my way
when I've got my groovewalk going. It's a rhythm
you learn:
move those ironzilla legs
to the cherry-berry vanillacream sparklepop
and your pneumafuel efficiency will increase
according to the Yakihatsu formula (sigma3, 9 to the power
 of four)

Robots are like Mars: they need
girls.
 Boys won't do;

the memesoup is all wrong. They stomp
when they should kiss
and they're none too keen
on having things shoved inside them.
    You can't convince them
there's nothing kinky going on:
you can't move the machine without IV interface
fourteen intra-optical displays
a codedump wafer like a rose petal
under the tongue,
silver tubes
wrapped around your bones.

    It's just a job.
Why do boys have to make everything
sound weird? It's not a robot
until you put a girl inside. Sometimes
                I feel like that.
                A junkyard
                the Company forgot to put a girl in.

I mean yeah.
My crystal fingers are laser-enabled
light comes out of me
like dawn. Bright orangecream
killpink
sizzling tangerine deathglitter. But what
does it mean? Is this really
a retirement plan?
    All of us Company Girls
sitting in the Company Home
in our giant angular titanium suits
knitting tiny versions of our robot selves
playing poker with x-ray eyes

crushing the teakettle with hotlilac chromium fists
every day at 3?

I get a break
every spring.
    Big me
powers down
transparent highly conductive golden eyeball
by transparent highly conductive golden eyeball.
    Little me steps out
and the plum blossoms quiver
like a frothy fuchsia baseline.
    My body is
    full of holes
where the junkbody metalgirl tinkid used to be
inside me inside it
and I try to go out for tea and noodles
but they only taste like crystallized cobalt-4
and faithlessness.
I feel my suit
all around me. It wants. I want. Cold scrapcode
    drifts like snow behind my eyes.
I can't understand
why no one sees the dinosaur bones
of my exo-self
dwarfing the ramen-slingers
and their steamscalded cheeks.

    Maybe I go dancing
    Maybe I light incense.
    Maybe I fuck, maybe I get fucked.
Nothing is as big inside me
as I am
when I am inside me.

When I am big
I can run so fast
out of my skin
my feet are mighty,
flamecushioned and undeniable.
  I salute with my sadgirl/hardgirl/crunchgirl
purplebolt tungsten hands
the size of cars
    and Saturn tips a ring.

It hurts to be big
but everyone sees me.

  When I am little
when I am just a pretty thing
and they think I am bandaged
to fit the damagedgirl fashionpop manifesto
instead of to hide my nickelplate entrance nodes
    well
I can't get out of that suit either
but it doesn't know how to vibrate
a building under her audioglass palm
until it shatters.

I guess what I mean to say is
I'll never have kids. Chances for promotion
are minimal and my pension
sucks. That's okay.
After all, there is so much work
    to do. Enough for forever.
And I'm so good at it.
All my sitreps shine
like so many platinum dolls.
I'm due for a morphomod soon—
I'll be able to double over at the waist

like I've had something cut out of me
and fold up into a magentanosed Centauri-capable spaceship.
    So I've got that going for me.
At least fatigue isn't a factor. I have a steady
decalescent greengolden stream
of sourshimmer stimulants
available at the balling of my toes.
    On balance, to pay for the rest
  well
you've never felt anything
like a pearlypink ball of plasmid clingflame
releasing from your mouth
like a burst of song.
    And Y Prefecture
is just so close by.

The girls and I talk.
  We say:
start a dream journal.
take up ikebana.
make your own jam.
  We say:
Next spring
let's go to Australia together
look at the kangaroos.
  We say:
turn up that sweet vibevox happygirl music
tap the communal PA
we've got a long walk ahead of us today
and at the end of it
a fire like six perfect flowers
arranged in an iron vase.

INK, WATER, MILK

Three things are happening at the same time.

It will be hard for you to believe—being only a reader with employment concerns and a jaded cultural consciousness and having limited patience for this sort of nonsense—that they are happening all at once. Not only at the same time, but in the same place. One on top of the other. Like three blue bowls nesting. Like three cells of film aligned atop a light box. If you will sit quietly inside the palm of my hand I will keep the wind out and we can watch the three things happen into each other. Like ink and water and milk. I will tell you the truth at the beginning so that you will recognize it in the end: there is nothing in this world but ink and water and milk. Of course it doesn't make any sense now. Three things are happening at the same time. There will be some natural seepage of cause and effect.

There. This is my hand. It is big enough. There are lines on it like anyone's hand. A ring. A short, straight scar underneath the pinky finger. Never mind how I got it. It is hard and twisted. The cut was deep. You can rest your tea on it and it will not fall over.

It would be best, really, if you could tell one thing, and I tell another, and a third person tell the third, so that our voices also happen at the same time, interleaving like fingers. But I do not ask for so much cacophony. I will tell them all and you will remember them thatched as tightly as a roof.

INK

A summer moon sits heavy as a buoy on Sagami Bay. Cicadas shriek at it, but it is placid. It bobs up and down on the still water. Among the bells of the real buoys, the soft bells of the moon go unnoticed. The sturgeons deep under the water hear them—and the giant clams.

Kyorinrin also hears the moon. Down in the green-black hills, where the camphor and the cassia and the plum and the red pine and the willow crowd together as close as commuters on the night train, he listens to the moon in an abandoned paper umbrella factory. The windows have holes in them like fists through frost. A hole in the roof sags and gapes like a mouth. The door is bolted and boarded, the pipes burst open like iron flowers, and a sign informs you that you may lease it, if you wish, from a holding company that was liquidated in 1976. The sign is freshly painted. White characters on a vermilion background. Himura Holding Company. Interested Parties Are Begged to Inquire. 075 871 7746.

Inside the paper umbrella factory the floor shines. Kyorinrin does his best to keep it livable. One thousand kerosene lamps burn, on every pallet, crate, employees' washbasin, manager's desk, inspection platform, dye sink, industrial lathe, glue vat, bank of lockers, cafeteria table, pile of ledgers, the gleaming floor. They burn during the day and the night, and they burn a deep shade of cyan. Their fuel is also cyan. There are actually only nine hundred eighty-one lamps. But one thousand is a better number.

Kyorinrin makes his home in the foreman's office. The roof there still keeps rain out. This is important because Kyorinrin is not a person but a large paper scroll. His pages look very old, darkened to a rich animal color. His roller is thick and bronze with a badger stamped on one end and a chrysanthemum on the other. His paper is blank, but that is a temporary situation.

Kyorinrin is not as old as he looks, but he likes to think he provides a sense of continuity. He came to the factory in 1950 in the personal effects of the first foreman, whose name, though unimportant to you and me, was Akiyama Isao. Kyorinrin lived for many years in a glass case along with other objects Akiyama found sacred in a certain private, personal way. These included two small silver rabbit figurines, a photograph of a girl named Akemi who died in the bombardment of Tokyo, a lock of his grandmother's hair cut on her wedding day, an airplane ticket to a place called Adelaide which Akiyama bought but did not use, a statuette of Jizo wrapped in a red scarf with a red cap on his smooth stone head, a Japanese-to-English dictionary, a miniature onyx elephant with a broken trunk, a map of ordnance sites in the mountains around Yokosuka, and Kyorinrin himself, who bore originally a professionally calligraphed genealogy of the Akiyama clan, inked on commission in 1910, the year Isao was born.

Kyorinrin supposes all these objects make a person, but you can never know very much from the inside of a glass case.

Like the rest of the umbrella factory, the case is broken now. The floor of the office still shimmers with a light snow of shards. Kyorinrin had had enough of silver rabbits and Adelaide and dead girls. He looks at it sometimes from the foreman's chair. Jizo still stands upright. One rabbit. The lock of hair.

Every evening Kyorinrin rolls luxuriously out to his full length across the factory floor. His paper exults in its own length. Every evening he causes a story to flow over his body in deep, profoundly black ink. Before the sun hefts up over the cinnamon trees, he bathes himself in the employees' basin and erases what he wrote. He uses the badger end of his roller to spray water down his creases, like an elephant with a working trunk.

The paper scroll does not live alone. Not anymore. He does not remember Tsuma coming, only that one day she was there where she had not been before. She is a kanji representing the word *wife*. Her brushstrokes are very fine. She stands thirty-three centimeters tall. Her ink is black like his own, though in the moonlight the edges of her glisten dark violet. She claims to have absconded from a large advertisement selling refrigerators. It was not an interesting life. Kyorinrin appreciates that.

"Today I am going to write a story about a white woman," announces Kyorinrin. The badger's bronze mouth moves when he speaks. His talk echoes.

Tsuma comes out from behind a dye sink crusted with bright pink stains. Violet ripples along her edges like electricity.

"Why would you want to do that?" she whispers.

WATER

A summer moon sits heavy as ballast on Uraga Harbor. Cicadas shriek at it, but it is unworried. It ripples in the quiet water. Among the mating of the cicadas the mating of the moon goes unremarked. The moon knows his own business—and his wife.

A fox who is not really a fox and an old woman who is not really an old woman also know the moon is in rut. They sit together under a persimmon tree high above the harbor. Fireflies dive and spiral around them, but the old woman keeps puffing up her cheeks and blowing them out. When her cheeks puff, they swell up bigger than green gourds and blush silver. The fox eats the fireflies, whether or not their tiny lamps are lit.

The old woman's name is Futsukeshibaba. She dresses in long white smoke that looks like a white kimono. Her obi is a length of dark water, flowing in a current around her bony waist. Her mouth is very red and her hair is longer than she is tall. It is the same smoke as her clothes. Her mouth glows in the white of her like fire. Futsukeshibaba blows out the lights of the world. That is the kind of creature she is. She desires only to blow out lanterns and lamps and candles. It is what she was made for. She has blown out the Emperor's personal lamp and would be happy to tell you about it. Once, she snuffed Issa's lantern when he fell asleep at his work, thereby saving his papers from the otherwise inevitable blaze. When she sees a flame, she yearns to put it out. It looks like a tear in everything to her, a ragged hole through which entropy can leak. Her breath is needle and thread.

Futsukeshibaba watches the blue-black water. She puffs up her cheeks, blows a sparrow out of the air with one quick cough, and hands it to the fox who is not really a fox because he is Inari, a god who wears his fox's body like it was a salaryman's suit. Inari crunches the bones in his fox-teeth. His fur gleams the color of saffron, the white tip of his great tail too much like a golden flame for Futsukeshibaba's comfort. She has already tried to blow it out several times, even though she knows better.

Inari and Futsukeshibaba are watching ships come into the harbor. They are not Japanese ships, but both the fox and the old woman knew that before they got here.

"What happens to the lights you blow out?" asks Inari, who possesses a great deal of curiosity about anatomy. "Where are they after you have extinguished them?"

"In my belly," Futsukeshibaba answers. She puts her hand there. "I eat them. They live in me forever as I do not generate waste. The inside of me looks like a festival night."

"But you hate the light so."

"I am sustained by the thing that violates my heart and breaks the peaceful dark of my mind. I thought you were a trickster god. Pretty standard riddle of existence."

"Does it taste good?"

"It tastes like the opposite of desire."

Inari accepts this. He thinks of the sweet incense of his shrine not far from here, of the electric green spiders in the paws of his statues.

"I don't know why you insisted we watch this," he sighs. His furry chest expands like a little sun and contracts again. "I'm bored, to be perfectly clear."

Prows glide into the harbor; sails and rigging luff and swing. Men sink anchor, secure lines, go about the work of making landfall. They are not Japanese men, but the fox and the old woman knew that before they got here.

"We don't have to stay. I know you are fond of the theater. It was meant as a gift."

Inari reaches up one paw and draws a persimmon out of the tree. It is not yet the time for persimmons. The fruit comes out like a drop of oil squeezed from a cloth, the branch bleeding orange, the wind groaning against the wood.

"If you hoped I would stop it—"

Futsukeshibaba interrupts. She does it so softly, like blowing out the fox's voice.

"Long ago I knew a blue paper lantern named Aoandon. She had a lilac-colored tassel with a pretty knot in it. She was rectangular. On one side of her a faded carp swam upstream. It used to be painted in real gold, but by the time I met her, only the outline remained, like a skeleton. I did not mind.

"Aoandon was not less accomplished than I. Her nature determined that she appear at storytelling festivals and competitions, a soft blue glow appearing when the last tale is told, lighting the way home. Once, she illuminated the midnight path of Murasaki Shikibu, whose sandals were very pale ash wood with charcoal silk straps that nested between her toes. Aoandon was always reluctant to admit that the great lady was tipsy with plum wine and ghost stories, but there it is. When she saw a darkness, she yearned to kindle it.

"I discovered her after a boasting tournament, guiding home a man who successfully claimed to have made love to every woman in a certain prefecture and left a different flower in each of their navels. He was so drunk he tried to seduce me. But I looked only at the blue paper lantern. Glowing as bright as the pole star. I wanted to blow her out. I wanted to eat her. I wanted her to exist in me forever. She looked at me with the eyes of her carp and we recognized immediately that we could so easily annihilate one another with the softest breath, the merest flicker. I could extinguish her, and she could burn me alive. The boastful man saw our intent gaze and ran."

"Obviously, you became enemies. Or did you blow her down right then, before she could strike?"

Futsukeshibaba shakes her head. The smoke of her hair wisps.

"That is a human game. We fell in love."

MILK

A summer moon sits heavy as a hand on Tokyo Bay. Cicadas shriek at it, but it does not answer. It makes a fist in the open water. Among the judgments of the city, the judgment of the moon goes unheard. The naval officers on watch suffer under it but have no name for it.

The woman walking the streets of Yoshikura does not hear it. She hears the cicadas, their mating sounds like engines screeching in her brain. She hears doors open and shut. She hears her own steps and the buzz of vending machines red and gleaming in the dark. She is not a Japanese woman. The machines anchor her new world. They tell her where she is—she lives suddenly in a place without numbers. There are no signs to tell her what a road is called or what the addresses of the houses might be. The vending machine closest to home has hot and cold coffee cans, a melon drink, milk tea, and large bottles of lemonade and cold tea. Most of the others don't have the bigger bottles, and she clings to this. For her, Japan is a series of sigils: a liter bottle of brown tea means home. The bus from the American base to her neighborhood has kanji that look to her like a princess's ball gown, a running dog, and the bars of a jail. But she has already met another Navy wife, a blonde woman who wears a great deal of khaki, who says that she takes that same bus, but the characters look to her like opera glasses, a typewriter, and the pillars of a country house. She told the other wife: *For foreigners, Japan is a Rorschach painting.* The blonde gave her a strange look and turned around to have a different conversation with the Captain's wife. The wives call each other by their husbands' ranks and their husbands' surnames. It is as though, without them there, they speak with their husbands' mouths.

She walks up—everything is up here. The houses terrace up through the hills, one on top of the other, like stacking bowls. She memorizes the vending machines along her path like a thread through a labyrinth. Green water bottles, candy, Coca-Cola products. The house she lives in now has another house inside it. As though it is pregnant. As though it is alive. The other house is meant for in-laws, closed up behind screens with snowy pines and serene partridges painted on them. A second living room, tiny and concealed behind a frozen pinecone. Hiding behind a clutch of partridge eggs, a second master bedroom, a second office. It unnerves her. It seems to say she should fill the other house with something. But she has nothing but herself. It is the nature of a naval officer to be absent. That is the kind of creature he is. When he sees a home, he longs to leave it. She loves him, she thinks, because he can destroy her.

She does not yet know what kind of creature she is. She is very young. Right now, she is a creature that interprets sigils, assigns them a private meaning until she can learn the public one. She is a creature walking at night in a green dress. The train goes by on elevated tracks somewhere far above her. She has begun to suspect she got married for the wrong reasons, and to the wrong person. But it's not important information. He isn't here and isn't going to be. She is as alone as she has ever been. She isn't married to a person. She is married to an empty house. To a country that is a stranger to her. To a house inside a house.

The woman turns the corner and stops short. Before her, a white tunnel opens up in the mountain. Cassia roots hang down in front of it. It seems to go nowhere and it seems to go on forever. Fluorescent lights fill up frosted plastic walls. Panels here and there have gone out, leaving long rectangles of black, lightless space. Bike paths line either side of the road through the tunnel. Electric green spiders spool down from the ceiling, flashing as they spin. She does not understand the tunnel. She does not have an explanation for it. She does not even know if she wants to go into it, to see where it goes. Like everything else, it is a sigil.

INK

Tsuma and Kyorinrin are lovers.

When they have been at each other, Kyorinrin must bathe a second time before sunrise. Once after his story, and once after his mate. The whole of his paper roll is covered with Tsuma. 妻 big and small, dark and ghost-grey, graceful and awkward—and growing sloppier as the night wears on. The characters are still wet when Kyorinrin washes them away. Wet and black and rimmed with another color, the color of raisins, the color of her love.

In the midnight center of his roll, one 妻 glows huge and deep and all violet, all glow. It is the 妻 of her climax. It is a secret 妻 only Kyorinrin knows. He looks at it a long time before he rinses it clear. It makes him think of new stories. It makes him think of the liquid sound of her, landing on his parchment body like a detonation.

Tsuma is shy except when she is inking him. It took her a long time to learn to say anything but her own name and the name of the refrigerator manufacturer. She still feels uncertain of her accent. But when she repeats herself against the body of Kyorinrin, she has no uncertainty. She knows how to say herself. She knows how to write herself.

"I am going to name her Akemi!" Kyorinrin rustles with excitement.

Characters appear on his body. Kyorinrin has beautiful penmanship.

"That is not a Western name," whispers Tsuma. "Your research is untidy."

"But I like the *sound* of Akemi. It doesn't matter anyway. I made her, so I own her. And I say what her name is." Kyorinrin darkens with writing. "I am going to make her lonely because that is true to life. Her husband went to war and left her. Akemi does not speak Japanese or read it either, so when she looks at kanji she makes up stories about it so that she can remember which bus to take home and whether the onigiri at the market has salmon in it, which she likes, or salted plum, which she does not like."

"Don't name her that, Kyorinrin."

"I have named the other wives after American first ladies. It will show up her sense of abandonment that she does not have a political name."

"All names are political." Tsuma toes the dust of the factory floor with the tip of one brushstroke.

"I am writing a story about a white woman who is writing a story about Japan. She writes her story because she is angry, so angry she is like a bull inside the skin of a person. Her horns pierce her from the inside. She writes her story to stand between her and her anger. I write my story because I am also angry."

"What are you angry about? I hope I have not—"

Kyorinrin interrupts her, and he does it so cleanly it is as though her voice has been erased.

"No, no, that is not what I mean." Writing moves more quickly over the surface of the scroll. "I am angry because I was left here. Because when the glass case broke I was the only one who jumped out. I was alone. I thought at least Jizo would be like me. Alive like me. I am angry because people will never come back to make umbrellas here on account of the ordnance buried quite nearby. I am angry because the war has been over for a long time but when

I decided to write a story about Yokosuka, the first thing I thought of was the American Navy. I am angry because I am hungry and the pink dye is almost gone."

Tsuma comes to him and touches the edge of his paper with the edge of her ink.

"It's all right," Kyorinrin whispers.

Tsuma eases down onto him. The shape of her blooms on his body. The bronze chrysanthemum on his roller moans with relief.

WATER

Inari is female now. She has no attachment to gender. The way some blush or sweat or yawn, that is the way Inari shifts between male and female and androgyne. She opens a basket and begins to pull out her mail to sort. Inari receives her mail once a week. It is a principal joy for her.

On the top of the mail basket crinkle the carbon papers of a gas bill. In addition to the gas bill, Inari has received a notice to appear in court for traffic violations, tax documents, a shipment of rice in individual two-kilogram red bags, a crate of kabocha squash, three pornographic magazines, a kit to build a radio-controlled mecha-warrior (decals, laser-axe, operator figurine, and a variety of canonical paint colors included), a Muji catalog, and seventeen issues of her favorite manga, none from the same series, as Inari reads widely and bores easily.

Time is not meaningful for Inari and Futsukeshibaba. They are watching an Admiral collect soil from the shore and put it in a crystal bottle for his comrades back home. They are watching trade negotiations stretching through the summer. They are watching the festival of the dead one hundred years from now light the bay with so many lanterns and scorch the sky with so many rockets that the city looks like the inside of Futsukeshibaba. They are watch-ing the capital come to Kamakura eight hundred years past. They are watching it leave again. Futsukeshibaba is watching Inari give birth, sometimes to foxes and sometimes to gods. Inari is watching Futsukeshibaba make careful love to a blue paper lantern in the Kyoto springtime. They are watching detonations. They are watching the new economy. They are watching the cherry blossoms in Tsukayama Park. They are watching the Yokohama BayStars play the Hiroshima Carp. They are watching girls dance in Roppongi under orange and blue lights. They are watching the cypress roofs of the royal residences burn. They are watching sailors sleep on the black ships in Uraga Harbor and they are watching Futsukeshibaba performing her duty during the war, keeping Tokyo dark while the sirens sing.

Inari holds up one of her pornographic magazines in her tail, whose tip blazes with pale fur.

"There is a piece of fiction in between the naked pictures here," she announces indignantly.

"This offends you?" answers Futsukeshibaba. "I have heard fiction pays better when nakedness is involved."

"Obviously I am not offended," snaps the fox-god. "I am the patron of writers. But in this story an American travels to Tokyo and gets drunk in Roppongi on loud fuschia drinks. But little does he know the beautiful woman in the white miniskirt dancing with him is Yuki-Onna, the vampire goddess of winter!"

"Too bad for him," smirks Futsukeshibaba. "She's going to freeze his pancreas and then dive down his throat to eat it."

Inari's fox eyes glitter. "*Ah*, but that is not what happens! Instead the American *fucks* Yuki-Onna and the fuck is so good she lets him live!"

Inari has a filthy mouth. She is a trickster; she cannot help it.

"Yuki-Onna is my sister! How dare this writer say that is a thing that could happen! She can't even fuck humans; their pitiful cocks cannot penetrate her because her hymen is made of polar ice. You cannot get inside her. You can only look at her right before she devours you. Leave it to these *things*," she gestures at the sleeping men in the ships below, "to not know the difference between eating and fucking."

Futsukeshibaba smiles to herself. She puts her hand on her belly where all the light she has ever consumed dwells.

"And why is Aoandon the blue paper lantern not with us tonight?" asks the fox-god, meaning to be cruel because the old woman did not give her an answer.

"She will leave me for a paper scroll in sixty years. We are not speaking right now. I will get over it. She will love him for the same reason that we love each other now: a blue paper lantern is a being of fire and a great scroll is made of paper and she will know she could destroy him with the merest blink of her cyan eye. But it will never be an equal match, because the scroll cannot harm her the same way. If he tried to smother her flame, he would only set himself ablaze. You can only truly love someone who can destroy you."

Together, Inari and Futsukeshibaba watch a scroll unroll himself and beg the blue paper lantern of his desire to remove her shade with the faded carp swimming on it. He begs her to bring her naked flame as close as he can bear it. On the body of the scroll, round scalds appear, rust-colored against his unblemished page. When he can take no more of it, he turns the chrysanthemum end of his bronze roller to her flame and lets her flicker against it until the carp shimmers gold and wriggles upstream.

"No one can destroy me," says Inari, as though she is considering it for the first time.

"I'm sure that's not true," answers Futsukeshibaba. She pats the fox's tail comfortingly.

Inari hopes that the radio-controlled mecha will be sturdy enough for her to wear when it is done. If she does not put the operator figurine inside, there will be room for a fox. So long as the kit experienced good quality control, Inari is confident she will be able to swing her laser-axe just like Junko, the Triumphant Neon Champion of Saturn.

MILK

Akemi stands inside the tunnel. She can see it doesn't really go nowhere. It goes on a long way, but there is a dark circle out there at the end which surely means it connects to the world again. Akemi's hair is soaked and knotted. She is from a cold city in the mountains—she has never known heat like this, heat that embraces you, clothes you, knows you intimately, suckles at you until you feed it on your sweat. The night beats blue and dark and Akemi feels full of that grasping, manic, gravityless sadness that always comes when she has not slept. She is full of books she might write. She is full of the next two years she will spend alone and she is full of her loneliness. She is full of the cicadas' scream. She has not cried. The other wives told her not to cry; it upsets the men when you cry.

She is full of little lights blowing out one by one by one.

Akemi imagines meeting someone else in the tunnel. Someone beautiful, someone unlike her. His name should be Taro, like the boy in the fairy tale. He could tell her how his parents longed for a child so deeply and the lack of one was such a wound to them that they went to a fertility clinic in Yokohama. In the lobby of the clinic a vending machine would have offered his mother and father peach candies, peach juice, peach tea, peach cookies, and pickled peach slices wrapped in cello-foil. The nurse might have brought them into a cold room with peach-colored walls and introduced herself as Momoko, which means "peach child." His mother would have laid down in a paper gown with cartoonish peach blossoms printed on it and stood with Taro inside her like a stone in a fruit. Akemi imagined liking this story enough to take Taro home and show him her nakedness in the house inside her house. It is a way she could destroy her husband, as he can destroy her. She has never had that power. She wants to be in a story like that, but the tunnel is empty.

Many years from now, Akemi will be unable to separate her marriage from Japan. She will not think of the time before it or after it. Japan will be the face of her husband. She will love Japan because it did not leave her. It did not accept her, but it did not leave her. His eyes will be the bays on either side of Yokosuka and his mouth will be a torii gate and his voice will be the schoolgirls on the train and her eyes will be the eyes of the women on a game show she watches on New Year's Eve, who must keep a perfect smile while battered from all sides with kitchen implements thrown by some offstage hand. And she will write about it forever and inside her writing about it the terrible simple sentence will repeat but never appear: *I hated my husband even before he left.*

INK

The moon has flown up and away to the other side of the hills. A lightening, a still blue change grows in the broken factory windows and everything is wet with the morning to come.

"Stop now," whispers Tsuma. "It is time to wash and to sleep."

"But I have adventures for her!" cries Kyorinrin. "I have made her discover seven pregnant American women eating squid tentacles fresh from the boil, ashamed of their craving but ravenous. I have made her too fat to fit into the kimono her friend has offered to dress her in so that both of them are humiliated and choose not to speak of it again. I have made her buy genetically modified watermelons in the shapes of cubes and stack them in her refrigerator to stare at but not eat because it is one strangeness too far. I have made her pregnant and then not-pregnant—I am considering letting her milk come in so that she cannot unknow what has happened. I have made her crawl into the storage boxes sunk into the floor of her kitchen, curl around herself and try to disappear into the earth—"

"Stop it!" cries Tsuma. It is the loudest sound Kyorinrin has ever heard her make. "Stop it! I don't want to hear about her! I don't want her wrong name or her sadness or her ignorant mawking at kanji or another story about a Western person in Japan pointing at everything and I don't want her aloneness, I don't want it, it's the size of her whole body, I don't want to look at it, I hate her, I hate her, I hate her!"

Tsuma cried bitterly and with every hitching sob *I hate her* she brought herself down hard on the body of Kyorinrin *I hate her* leaving 妻 over and over *I hate her* big and deep and wobbling, 妻 妻 妻 *I hate her*.

Kyorinrin gasps and wheezes and it is pleasure and it is pain. When it is over he curls his paper over his mate and her ink seeps through to the other side of him and she weeps the strange tears of kanji, uncontrollable, indelible.

In the end there is nothing left of Akemi but 妻.

WATER

"You can blow out a sparrow," Inari says. It is not a question.

"Yes. It's no different. What lights us, what lights wood, what lights oil." Futsukeshibaba braids the smoke of her hair. The sun is restless, lining the bay with lavender, eager for the events of the day to begin their occurring.

"If I ask you to blow out the Admiral and his men, will you do it?"

Futsukeshibaba thinks about it. "No," she sighs. "I could not bear to keep them all inside me."

"I didn't really mean it. It's already happened and this is the fourth time we've watched it. I was only curious what you would say." Inari looks up at the dimming stars, the bats flapping over the cassia trees. "The trick when writing about Westerners," she sighs, "is to pretend they are unhuman. Like us or like the opposite of us if we have an opposite. Otherwise the tale is too sad to finish. These are good seats. I thank you for the gift."

Behind them a cool blue light pours out like a cup of water. Futsukeshibaba smiles.

"At the end of storytelling," she says. "That's her time."

Aoandon leans against the shoulder of her lover. The blue paper lantern will light the way home for the fox and the old woman and she will not say anything about how petty it is to fight about an infidelity that she will not even contemplate for another sixty years. Her carp looks at the smoke of Futsukeshibaba's kimono and kindles gold with longing. The blue fire in Aoandon burns steady and strong. She is not intimidated by Inari. She lit the way for Ama-no-Uzume to come home from dancing the sun goddess to life again. She knows foxes can see quite well in the dark anyway.

"You know that I could end you with a snap of my jaws." Inari says this cheerfully, and it is also not a question.

"Yes," says Futsukeshibaba. She smiles wider.

Below them the sailors have wakened. They eat, they stretch, pop the bones of their spines, look for orders, square cargo, prepare landing parties. Jellyfish clot around the ships, their simple rings and veils staring dumbly up at the masts, the men, the cannons.

Gently, Futsukeshibaba lifts Inari's heavy tail. It is as big around as the pillar of a temple, the color of persimmons. She does it so the blue paper lantern of her heart can see it, and she does it with her eyes locked on the eyes of the fox-god. With infinite satisfaction, Futsukeshibaba blows out the light at the end of Inari's tail.

MILK

There is a school of bonsai-cutting that, should part of a tree die or wither, preserves the dead material and incorporates it into the life and sculpture of the bonsai. The tree itself lives, but there is a dead thing in it. It lives around its dead part. The death becomes part of the beauty of the tree until the tree could not be beautiful without it. It is difficult—there is always the danger of the death spreading and taking hold. You cannot remove the death from the tree. That would be dishonest. It would be pretending that the death had never come near. You must be vigilant, keep the dead wood clutched tight so that the slow decay fuels everything else. So that it communicates effectively the impermanence of all.

Akemi is pruning a tree. Her teacher is named Fusao. She has no hope that she will show any talent here. She cannot even bring herself to make the first cut. It seems too monumental a choice.

At the base of the trunk, there is already a scar. A sigil. It will grow before she notices it, spreading like frost. A death in the shape of a kanji:

妻

FIFTEEN PANELS DEPICTING THE SADNESS OF THE BAKU AND THE JOTAI

WHAT SHE WHISPERED

When you, sweet sleeper, wake in the morning, one arm thrown over your golden-sticky eyes, sheets a-mangle, your dreams still flit through you, ragged, full of holes. You can remember the man with the yellow eyes, but not why he chased you. You can remember the hawk-footed woman on your roof, but not what she whispered.

That is my fault. I could not help it. I tromped through you in the night and ate up your dreams, a moth through wool. I didn't want them all, only the sweetest veins, like fat marbling a slab of ruby meat, the marrowy slick of what she whispered, why he ran.

I am a rowling thing—my snout raises up toward the moon to catch the scent of your sweat. I show my flat teeth to the night wind. I beg permission of your bedclothes to curl up in the curve of your stomach, to gnaw on your shoulders, your breasts, your eyelids. I must open up a hole in you, to crawl through to the red place where your dreams spool out.

You put your arm around me in the night. Do you remember? My belly was taut and black, a tapir's belly, a tapir's snout snuffling for your breath as a pig for truffles. You were my truffle, my thick, earthy mushroom. You were delicious, and I thank you for my supper.

A JEWEL WE MAY NOT GNAW

At dawn, blue light shines on my woolly stump-tail. I catch the tin-patched 6:17 commuter train from your house to my home, deep in the Paradise of the Pure Land. My friend Yatsuhashi lumbers on board at your aunt's house, the one with the wide white porch. She is fat and full of your aunt's dreams of straddling her supervisor while he recites Basho. She takes her seat in the empty car; I take mine. She sits up and her tapir body unfolds neatly along three creases to become the body of a respectable businessman in a respectable black suit. I, too, unfold and straighten my tie. The attendant brings cups of hot, sweet *matcha*, but we refrain, straining at the pelt with the night-feast. If you saw us, you would not think we had snorted and snuggled against you all through the dark and moony hours. You would think: *There go two wealthy and reputable gentlemen, off to their decent, clean desks in the city.*

But we have worked our shifts already, and we aim toward home, hurtle toward it, home to the peach tree of immortality and the pearl-troughs of enlightened discourse, where we will disgorge our meals for the pleasure of eating them again.

"Kabu," says Yatsuhashi, though she knows my full name is Akakabu. She insists on the familiar because she has no manners. "Do you think that dreams taste more like cherries or more like salmon roe? I can never decide."

"With respect, Yatsuhashi-san, the comparison with roe is not at all apt. Recall that at the bottom of a dream is a hard jewel we may not gnaw, the jewel of the sleeping soul, clung with dream-meat and sugar. Roe is sweet and soft and bursts on the tongue in a shower of golden salt—how rare is the roe-dream! Only the very young and the very old have no pit on which we may break our teeth if we are not careful."

"Of course you are right, Kabu. But I cannot escape the feeling of fishiness; the dreams of sex-starved aunts wriggle in me so!"

That is my friend's way of talking. Many Baku talk like this, because they are not sensible, and all they eat all night are the kinds of dreams which do not agree with a tapir's stomach: drunken dreams, fever dreams, sickness dreams, the dreams of enfeebled children. These are so rich it is hard to resist, like a tiny table set with a cake so moist it wets the cloth, but they make a Baku babble and walk into walls.

Disembark for Yokosuka-Chuo Station.

The mechanical voice is slim and soft and breathy, a dream-voice. I approve. I obey.

THE PARADISE OF THE PURE LAND

Does it surprise you that Pure Land has a train station? It has many. We are subtle, we who inhabit this place—not only Baku but many other beasts and *tsukumogami* and dragons and maidens with the moon in their hair and bodhisattva with bare feet. We let humans build grey, stocky towers in the Gardens of Right Practice; we let them bring great gun-bristled ships to the Lotus Harbor; we let them pave the Avenue of Yellow Smoke and set up pachinko parlors there. We let them call Pure Land Yokosuka, and we watched the Butterflies of Perfect Thought sizzle on the neon of their night-club advertisements. We were clever—we are safe, a dream in their sleeping, hidden beneath a human city, where no one, not even their soldiers with golden buttons, will ever think to look for heavenly pavilions.

It is not that there is no sadness in the Paradise of the Pure Land. On the contrary, we must all report for sadness once in our long, endless, peach-saturated lives, so that we may have something hard and terrible to hold against the beauty of the Pure Land. No one likes to talk about their sadness, but we have all reported on schedule and done our duty. I want to tell you about mine, I want you to dream about it, but manners make it difficult to get to the point.

I have an apartment above Blue Street in the Paradise of the Pure Land. The street does not really have a name—it has a number—but the humans thoughtfully paved it with sparkling blue stones, perhaps in some instinctive nod to our tastes, and so we and they call it Blue Street, for we are all of us together sagacious folk. From its window I can see the bay, the green water foamed with trash so that each wave is tipped with beer bottles, cellophane, detergent boxes, swollen manga, orange rinds. Beneath the surface is an improbable depository of bicycles, dumped by poor souls who could not parse out the arcane laws of garbage removal—our nature does shine through in places, and complexity of order is paramount in the pure land of contemplation. Jellyfish tangle in the wheel spokes, confused, translucent, lost.

I am lost too. I have mistaken a bicycle wheel for safe harbor. No one is perfect.

CLOSE YOUR EYES

It would be better if you closed your eyes. I relate more easily with the sleeping. If you could dream my story, I could lumber along the low river of your spine, snuffling out the parts which are too horrible, too radiant, too private for your witness. I could eat them weeping into your brain-pan, and you would wake remembering only salt.

I don't suppose you are tired. No? Ah, well.

Suffice it to say I loved a creature, and that creature is no more. It is the sort of thing dreams were invented to wrangle.

BASHFULNESS OR THE NIGHT WIND

My love was owned by a white woman. She and I met at work, as all modern lovers do, while I was on my nightly rounds. I had curled into the white woman's arms and fixed my teeth to her mouth, working at her throat, pulling up the jellied marrow of her little housely terrors. Westerners do not have the most complex palette. She dreamed of a husband in a white uniform, a husband with a sword at his hip and also an oily black gun, a cap of gold, eyes of silver. The husband touched the sea and it glowed phosphorescent green, sickly. He did not smile at her; I ate his smile.

I saw her over the shoulder of the sad little wife. She was tall and dark, standing in the corner as though she guarded her mistress's sleep. Her figure was angular, her expression still as a soldier's. Rafu, my Rafu! How I have pored over that first glimpse, held it in my paws, packed it into a box with tears and red tissue, taken it out to warm me when the stars had frozen!

I rested my chin on the Western woman's shoulder, gazing at the golden-black thing that I did not yet know was Rafu. She bowed slightly. Her hinges creaked. The silk of her panels fluttered slightly in bashfulness or the night wind. A willowy green slip hung half over her face—my Rafu was a folding screen, a silk monster of beauty like statues. A *Jotai*, a screen so old that one day she woke up and had a name and an address and an internal monologue. You earn these things after one hundred years or so. The world owes them to you, if you survive it.

"What are you doing here, glory-of-the-evening, in this pretty pale devil's house?"

Rafu fluttered again. There were golden tigers playing on the silk where her thighs might be. They batted at floaty, cloud-bound kanji like mice.

TO CONCEAL HER FROM HER LIFE

"Her name is Milo," whispered my not-yet-beloved screen. "Her father wanted a boy. I was a present from her friend Chieko, who chose in her youth to be kind to the Navy wives because they are worse than children: mute, lost, dead, rigid with stupidity, which is their only defense. Chieko loved *mikon* oranges and had a mole on her left breast. Once a boy kissed it without permission under a persimmon tree, and Chieko never forgot it—she burned warmer and brighter in that moment than she ever did again. Her mother Kayo, whose favorite perfume was made from lotus and lemon water, who had a husband whose face was always red and three miscarriages only I witnessed—I never told anyone—bought me from a teahouse in Yokohama, where I belonged to a little girl who turned into an old woman as if by magic. She was called Masumi and all her kimono were pink with black cherry blossoms. She drank in secret, squatting in the secret shade of me, drinking silver things until she was sick. Her great-aunt, Aoi, loved a man from England who did not love her back, and so she married a ginger farmer whose fingers burned her, and had no children. Aoi found me in a shop in Kamakura, by the sea, and thought that I would suffice to conceal her from her life.

"I have had much time to consider women. Milo is no worse than any of them."

"Her dreams taste thin and bitter, like the white membranes of limes."

Rafu shrugged, a peculiar raising and dropping of her slats. "She is sad. She does not speak Japanese. Her husband went to the desert months and months ago. Every day she goes to the market and brings back chocolate, a peach, and a salmon rice-ball for her dinner. She sits and eats and stares at the wall. Sometimes she watches television. Sometimes she walks three miles to Blue Street to look at necklaces in the window that she wishes someone would buy for her. Sometimes she walks along the pier to see the sunken bicycles, pinged into ruin by invisible arrows of battleship-sonar, crusted over with rust and coral. She likes to pet people's dogs as they walk them. That is her whole life. What should she dream of?"

"Something better."

DANCING DOWN THE WINDOWS

It is not that I thirsted for Milo's dreams. I could have had better from any rice-cooker salesman on Blue Street, marbled with darkness and longing for kisses like maple sap. But Rafu stood in the shadows of Milo's house, wrapped in the grassy yellow-green perfume of new tatami, showing the stars through her skin, laughing when I told her the jokes Yatsuhashi had snorted to me on the morning train. I rocked on my haunches below her and showed her all the things I could be: tapir, tiger, salaryman, shadow, water.

I forgot to fix my mouth to the sailor's wife. Her sawdust-dreams did not glisten. She cried in her sleep, chasing ships I wished to know nothing of, lost in her tired colonial despair.

I lost weight, as lovers will do.

On the seventh night I knew my Rafu, I unfolded into a silk screen with lonely tapirs drinking from a moonlit stream painted on my panels. I wanted so to please her. We stood side by side, saying nothing, content. Delicate snow came dancing down the windows. Milo slept on her mat below us and did not see our still, silent lovemaking.

"I can do that too," said Rafu coquettishly, when we had finished and sweat shone like water on our screens. "I can fold up into a tapir, a tiger, a salaryman, shadow, water. A girl."

"Show me!"

"Not yet," she demurred.

BECAUSE OF HER NAKEDNESS

"Come away from this tailless old alley cat," I begged my Rafu, resplendent in the night, golden against the dark. "I have an apartment above Blue Street. I will never throw clothing over you. I will show you the secret Peacocks of Right Intention, who make their nests in the Admiral's mansion and peck at him when he orders his men to stand in ridiculous lines and speak the nonsense of demon-kind. He cannot see them—the poor man thinks he has eczema. It is an excellent joke. I will take you walking through the Carnival of Right Livelihood, and we will eat black sugar burnt in the Ovens of Contentment. You can take the Baku-train with me every night and continue your study of women—I will eat only the dreams of women for your sake! Into the pachinko parlors we will go, hoof in hinge, and in the plinking of those silver balls we alone will hear the clicking movements of stars in perfect orbit and know that nothing is chance."

Rafu blushed—her panels blossomed with scarlet as though she could bleed. Milo snored and turned over in her sleep, murmuring in phantom agony, her brown hair caught in her wet mouth. Rafu watched her, tipping slightly toward the woman.

"No, Akakabu, passion of my elderly years! I love her. I love her, and I will never leave her."

"How can you love such a thing?"

"I love her because of her nakedness, Kabu. She has stood before me and peeled off all her clothes until she was utterly defenseless, her breasts and her shoulders and her lonely sex all for me, for my view, my love, my pity. I know that she had her tongue pierced when she was a girl but took it out when she married. I know that her right breast is somewhat larger than her left, that she has a birthmark at the base of her spine as though someone punched her, and that she has stretch marks on her belly, but no children, for there is nothing here for her to do but eat. These are such precious things to know! I knew them about Chieko, and Kayo, and Masumi, and Aoi too. They all showed me their bodies, and how the world stamped itself onto them. I have not even seen your body the way my mistresses show me theirs. She has been naked before me, Kabu, and I will not abandon a naked girl to the cold."

FIRST LADIES

I admit I was angry, that it was my fault in the end. I begrudged Rafu her naked women, her secret lovemaking in lonely houses full of women who would never see the green and purple of the Peacocks of Right Intention. I wanted to show my Jotai that a Baku, too, can know a human that way, and better, for no one is ever so naked as in their dreams, where everything shameful and bright glistens like sweet fat over bone.

I curled up into Milo's heavy sleeping arms, snarling at Rafu, gloating, taking up that flaccid Western mouth in mine and sucking down all her old, buried things, her grief and her loneliness and her cream-thick guilt, her tawdry affair in Okinawa, her lost lover who used to kiss her toes as though she were an angel that might confer blessing. I ate it all, greedily, slovenly. I ate her husband who left her, his sword and his gun and his curling, saluting smile. I writhed against Milo, my black tapir belly taut with her, hard and swollen, grinding into her, sliding off of the hard little cherry pit at the base of her dreams, scraping at it, breaking my teeth on the stone of her soul.

Rafu turned away from me in shame.

Milo wrapped her arms around me and opened her eyes. "All the other wives have First Ladies' names," she whispered, her voice sand-slurred with sleep. "Hillary, Laura, Eleanor, Pat, Libby. What's wrong with me?"

"You were supposed to be a boy," I said cruelly, because I chose to be cruel. "If you had been born as you were meant to, you would get to march about with a fine rifle and shoot at things and drink whiskey and have a lovely time, and no one would ever have left you."

"Oh," Milo said with finality, as though it had finally been explained to her satisfaction. She fell asleep again.

CREATURES OF STOMACH

I am sure it has happened before. We are creatures of stomach, after all. My mother told me when I was small and spotted that the first Baku was nothing but a great violet-translucent stomach, maybe with a bit of esophagus, and it floated over rooftops on stormy days, descending to cover sleepers like a blanket and draw up all their dreams into itself with perfect retention. In those days, no one remembered their dreams at all, so deft was the Baku in its slurping of them.

That Baku surely was blameless, but I am not. I ate too much Milo; I was so full of her my hiccups turned into anchors and dolphins and swam away through the night. Rafu rustled disgust—her gold flushed a jaundiced yellow, so deep was her disapproval of my gluttony.

I only did it to hurt you, my silken love, my Rafu, my vanished adored. I think that makes it better.

I tottered on my fat paws, skidding on the slick tatami, drunk, queasy. My skin felt too thick; I wanted to take it off, to go naked before Rafu and be loved as the women in her life had been. I deserved that, didn't I? I careened into a wooden candlestick, bounced off of a low table of red wood, bruised my snout on Rafu's corner; she clattered to the floor.

I threw up on the grass mats and lolled in my decrepitude beside my waste.

THE UNRUSHED FAMILIARITY OF A HUSBAND

A man lay on the floor. The substance of my retching. I vomited up Milo's dream, and it lay on the floor in a white uniform streaked with the silvery stuff of my digestion: tears, the honey of lost days, sweat, night-semen. His officer's cap tumbled off onto the tatami; his hair was wet and matted like a newborn's.

He stirred; Rafu held her slats together in terror, as silent as she could be. The man crawled to Milo's sleeping shape and curled into it as I had done, with the unrushed familiarity of a husband, or a frequent Baku. He kissed her hair, left streaks of silver on her neck. I watched from the shadows as he called her name and she rolled into waking, rolled into him, her face unfolding into a smile as I sometimes unfold into a man.

"How are you here?" she marveled, as well she might.

"I missed you," he murmured, slurred, unsure of English, as well he might be, having been in my stomach a moment previously. *Liar*, I thought.

"I've been so lonely," Milo sighed. "I hate it here. Can't we go home?"

"Yes, of course. Tomorrow." He was not listening to her. The sailor pulled at her frumpy nightgown, pulling her greyish, threadbare underthings away, pulling his sex from his crisp white trousers, clung with silvery dream-glue. She moaned a little, frightened, half-asleep yet.

"It's so strange," he gasped as he thrust awkwardly into her, with all the grace of an elephant falling upon a hapless antelope. "I was in the desert just a moment ago. Everything smelled like oil and sand. There were men on a raft; they shot at us, and all around them the sea was angry, blue and green, phosphorescent with spilled fuel and algae. It glowed, and the men's faces were so hollow."

Milo began to cry silently. Her body lurched with his motion.

"We shot back, we had to. I pulled their bodies out of the glowing water." He started to laugh roughly, pushing faster against her. "And it was so weird, their skin just came off in my hands, like a coat. So soft, like they were made of nothing, with nothing inside, and all we pulled out was skin and blood, no men at all."

"Don't laugh, it scares me," whispered Milo.

Her husband put his hands against her ears as if to blot out the sound of his laughter, which spiraled up and higher and further and faster, until water came from his mouth and his hands, water pouring into her, the salt-sea scouring her, shells and fish and sand and blood splashing out of him, into her ears, into her womb, into her mouth. She spluttered, coughed—he pushed the sea through her, and her lips became as blue as the waves, her hair streamed like kelp, his fingers left purple anemones on her ribs.

"Aren't you happy I'm back? Why don't you kiss me? Don't you love me?"

And he kissed her, over and over, wet, salty smacks in the dark, and above the sound of them I could hear Rafu crying, huddled like discarded furniture against the concrete wall.

YOU CAN'T LOVE MEAT

The dream-vomit sat cross-legged on the floor, waiting for someone to serve him tea. Milo lay broken by him, her face swollen, water dribbling from her mouth.

"Your name is Kabu. Akakabu," he said slowly to me. A child might well know its father. "Is my name Lieutenant?"

"No." I walked out of the shadow of the American television stand and sat on my haunches next to him. "Your name is Gabriel Salas, but you're not him, not really."

"No, I know that. If I were Gabriel Salas I would still be in the desert, and the sea would be glowing, and I would be able to see cities in the distance, full of crumbling and canny birds."

"You're a dream. Do you understand that?"

"Whose dream?"

"Your wife's. Look at what she dreams you will do to her, and what you have done in her dreaming."

The dream-sailor looked down at his wife. His expression was blank. "I loved her."

"Yes."

"I don't love her anymore. You can't love meat."

"That's your business."

"What do I do now, Akakabu?"

"This is the Paradise of the Pure Land. You might start with Right Thought. This is also Yokosuka. You might start with burying your wife and lighting incense for her."

"That does not sound like something I would do. Instead, I am hungry."

"You are hungry because you came out of me, and I am always hungry."

"I am going to the city, then. To eat things I like."

"What sort of things do you like?"

Lieutenant Gabriel Salas cocked his head thoughtfully to one side. He picked up his officer's cap and put it on. "Peacocks. Butterflies. Black sugar. Right Thought."

He strode from the house, his spine straight and proud, his steps turning south toward Blue Street.

When he had gone, Rafu crawled from the corner of the room, her slats digging into the tatami. As she dragged herself the slats of fine dark wood became fingers breaking their nails on the woven grass, her silk screens became shoulders, a stomach, a strong back. She stood up, unfolding into a woman with long, hinged arms, accordioning out from her sweet torso in hanging, tiger-painted screens that ended in graceful hands. She sank down over Milo's drowned body.

"Save her," my Rafu wept. "Save her because of her nakedness, how bare she was before me, and how I loved her smaller breast."

"It's no good, concealer-of-my-heart. I only know how to eat things."

BECAUSE YOU ARE NEW

The Paradise of the Pure Land exists within Yokosuka as hair caught in a brush—the teeth of the city rise tall through the tangles and think nothing of them, but deep in the comb, long onyx strands wind and snarl. It is, of course, possible to yank all these strands free with a pitiless fist. They will not protest.

Rafu and I followed the dream of Gabriel through Yoshikura-Chuo and along the highway, through the wet, dank tunnel and up the jungled terraces. He was not hard to follow, being loud and foreign. He ate cherry trees along the way, opening his jaw and swallowing them whole as I might. When he reached the city, he seized in one hand a Peacock of Right Intention, squirming blue and green, and in the other a young girl coming home from a date with an enlisted American on the sprawling grey base. He shoved each into his mouth like two legs of one golden chicken.

On Blue Street, he ate hats, belts, rice-cookers, kerosene lamps, light bulbs, expensive Italian shoes, the Grocers of Perfect Balance, aquariums, streetlamps, Prostitutes of Pure Mind, the Motorcycles of Holy Judgment. Rafu wrinkled her new nose and clapped her screen-arms.

"Is this what you are like, on the inside?" she said.

"This is what everyone is like on the inside," I sighed.

"It's not what I'm like!"

"That is because you are new. You did not have a stomach for one hundred years. You are only just learning how to fill it. You do not yet know it can never be filled."

Just ahead of us, the dream-Gabriel unhinged his jaw and swallowed a drink machine. It expired with a red whine.

"Will he eat us all?"

"Yes," I said calmly. "He is a dream; he does not know this is not a dream. His real self is somewhere impossibly hot, dreaming of his soft, plain wife who is not named after a First Lady. He eats up the world with a grey boat and a fine cap. Dreams are more literal. More honest."

"Why are you not afraid?"

"Because I know a thing about the Pure Land he does not."

Rafu took my tapir-form into her screen arms and kissed my ardent snout. I unfolded into a man in her arms, to match her, to please her. I wanted so to please her.

A PERFECT SHARD OF GOLD

There is no more sacred place in the Pure Land of Yokosuka than the pink palaces of the pachinko parlors. I would have taken Rafu there, to meditate with me in the blue haze of the electronic screens and the heady cigar smoke. Here, the bodhisattvas practice Right Gambling, prone before the unyielding goddesses of luck, their throats ecstatic and bare.

One by one, the dream-Lieutenant ate the goddesses from the ceiling, the green-limbed seraphs of Perfect Chance, sucking their toes down into his throat. Their screams were shattered by the crash and fall of silver balls. The old, shrunken men turning the wheels of the glittering machines did not move—they see nothing of the Pure Land, even when the sun rises over the harbor and grants each citizen of the Right City a perfect shard of gold. He is a dream; I am a dream; we are all dreams, and the flashing arcade lights blind them.

Gabriel laughed, a thick, fatty sound, a gargle, a chortle. The parlor erupted in jackpots and high scores. The goddesses who held back and gave forth at their whim had gone into his great, insatiable belly and held back no more.

"Please," said Rafu softly. The old men shouted for joy, jostled each other, shook fists at the perplexed proprietor. Rafu's voice barely sounded among them, but Gabriel turned toward her in hunger, his lips scarlet with secret blood.

"Do you remember," said Rafu, sliding toward him, "how Milo's toe was broken when she was six, running too fast after her friends through the forest behind her house? How it is still crooked, and aches, and how you used to rub it for her during thunderstorms until she was well? Do you remember how her waist curved so sweetly in, how her mouth tasted, how even when she had the flu she smelled like childhood to you, clean and innocent and permanent?"

"No," growled the dream-Gabriel.

"Do you remember how her fingers still had calluses, even

though she stopped playing the guitar so long ago? How her hair looked when it was tangled, when it was smooth? How her belly sloped, how her birthmark looked, how her ears curved?"

"No," growled the dream-Gabriel. "Instead, I want to eat you. Then I'll remember those things."

"Why are you doing this?"

Gabriel shrugged. "What else is there to do when you visit a foreign country?"

He turned to bite down on a crippled old woman with a cane and a bend in her back like a stair. Her skinny arms were full of silver pachinko balls. She was winning, of course she was winning. His invisible teeth shattered on her dry old skull, scraping off her jaw. She smiled quietly to herself.

"There is a pit in every dream that cannot be eaten," I said to Rafu. I was so tired. This was a lesson for baby Baku. "It will break you if you try it. Naturally it is the most delicious thing in a dream, and we have all had to learn to curb our desire for it. And in the dream of the Pure Land, the dream Yokosuka dreams waking and sleeping, an old woman sits in a pachinko parlor, our indestructible core, indestructible because she does not know she is the sweetest thing in the world."

The dream of Gabriel was breaking apart, spilling the silver dream fluid onto the floor, shuddering, shaking, crying out for help. I did not care.

But Rafu opened her arms to him, and ah, I should have known—we are each slaves to our own natures, even in the Paradise of the Pure Land, especially here, and if I know only how to eat, she knows only how to conceal, how to hide a thing from shame. Her arms flipped open, square screen by square screen, and she enveloped him so suddenly he could not move, clapped him up entirely in herself, all wall of golden Rafu.

The dream-Gabriel sobbed in her grasp. The things he had devoured began to tear out of him: hats, belts, rice-cookers, kerosene lamps, light bulbs, expensive Italian shoes, the Grocers of Perfect Balance, aquariums, streetlamps, Prostitutes of Pure Mind, the Motorcycles of Holy Judgment. The Seven Goddesses of Perfect Chance. They burst from him in his weakness—and burst through the body of Rafu, which was no more than silk, not really, leaving her skin hanging, ragged, torn threads fluttering in the breeze of falling silver.

THEN I WOKE UP

It was only a dream. Sometimes they say that, at the end of stories, in the land where Milo was born. *And then I woke up—it was only a dream.*

Stories here do not end like that. I cannot wake up. I do not sleep.

Milo cannot wake up. If she could, she would see in her house: a low table of red wood, several windows, a television, chocolate, a peach, a salmon rice-ball, and her friend Chieko's screen, shattered as though a cannonball had struck it, in a broken pile on the tatami. If she could wake up, she would have to get a new one—they can always get a new anything, these humans.

Only you can wake up, out of all of us, and be relieved. You can assure yourself that we never really existed, that Yokosuka is only a broken old military town, that folding screens never speak with voices like thread spooling. I will leave it all intact for you.

I am fasting now, anyway. I have my penance to pay.

Yet eating dreams is an essential act of waste management in the Paradise of the Pure Land. I did my duty. I swallowed the wreckage of the dream-vomit I spilled out of myself, and also the wreckage of Milo, sodden with seawater. I cleaned everything up, don't you see? It's all just the way it was before.

On the 6:17 commuter train, Yatsuhashi told me a joke about a geisha who wouldn't wear her wig. It rambled and was not funny. Yatsuhashi-san is an idiot. The apartment above Blue Street is empty because she is gone. She was never here, of course—I never brought her to my threshold, I never served her tea with the exquisite abasement of which I am capable. I never showed her the jellyfish. But once there was a glowing cord between our houses, hers tatami-golden and tall, just down the hill from Anjinsuka Station, mine clean and neat as dreams cannot be, polished with a spongey, devoted snout. But in dreams, one can feel the absence of a thing that never was, and so can I.

Rafu will never come here now; the emptiness is permanent.

The Paradise of the Pure Land remains. It is bigger than all of us and notices nothing. It sprawls by the sea, a reef of light, and as I trundle down the leaf-strewn length of Blue Street, the whole of the Pure Land turns to you as if to say something, something important, something profound.

And then you wake up. After all, it is only a dream.

GHOSTS OF GUNKANJIMA

Gunkanjima, or Battleship Island, is a tiny island in Nagasaki Prefecture on which coal was discovered in 1810. A boom followed, and the island was heavily populated and owned from seabed to rooftop by the Mitsubishi Corporation. At one point it was the single most densely populated area on the planet, before or since. Everything was imported to the island, including building materials—not even a blade of grass grew there. Japan's first concrete buildings were erected to house workers, who tunneled deep under the sea to find the vital coal. Eventually over-population and dwindling output began the island's decline—in 1974 it was permanently closed by Mitsubishi Corp. All remaining workers were sent elsewhere. Today, it is forbidden to all visitors and is being slowly reclaimed by nature.

During WWII, some 1,300 Chinese and Korean slave laborers died there.

The wind here always tasted like metal.

Xiao, Xiao, come to bed. The stair-ferns are soft; the stars are coming through the walls like mice.

* * *

The wind here always tasted of metal, steel come clattering up through the rotten slats of the bridges.

Xiao, the mushrooms have made pillows of the tatami—lay your head next to mine and stop this. No good comes from remembering it.

The wind here always tasted of metal, steel come clattering up through the rotten slats of the bridges strung like laundry between towers, a wheel of knives carving my arches.

Xiao, the old soggy suitcases have opened up; they are packed with grasses and fishtails wizened to moth's wings. Come fold yourself up with me like a shirt—the sleeve of me longs for the cuffs of you.

* * *

The air moves through itself with pointed toes, each foot creaking a slab of wood, a slab of step in the latticework of bridges and ladders and staircases that connect a city without roads. Up and down the air goes, a tightrope performer with a net of stone, a net of buildings whose teeth have long shattered and fallen out, leaving only jagged crowns to catch the creaking wind. The sound echoes until it strikes the seawall and is swallowed.

The air smoothes its hands on a sightless skirt. It whistles through a window without glass and stares at a bottle left standing, as if someone meant to come back for it. The dust on it is thick as soil. The room is crowded with stale breath, breath reeking of coal dust and seaweed and tobacco and unwashed socks. The air remembers that the Kim brothers lived here before they drowned, all seven of them, in a six-tatami hovel at the top of a tower. They had pimples and kept a cricket as a pet. They fed it pig-gristle carefully culled from seven dinners.

A sewing machine does not protest the delicate spiders which stitch their webs over its casing. There is no chirping in the corner, but the air hears it anyway.

* * *

Hsin. Wake up. It is time to go to work.

Work? Watching paper dissolve to dirt? Watching spectacles rust? The coal is gone; there is nothing to dredge up. Why don't we go down to the east wall and watch the tide strangle the shore?

Hsin. If you do not get up you will be punished. You are assigned to the sea-shaft today—that's twelve bridges across the roofs and all those stairs, all those stairs down to the mine mouth. And there is rain.

Xiao, pretty sparrow-wife, who will punish me? The foremen are gone, everything is gone, there are only the quiet termites boring through banis-ters, and they do not care if we are tardy.

Please, please wake up. I am tired too, my bones are full of black too, my spine wavers in me like a flapping flag, but I am ready, I am going to my assignment. We must make the best of it.

No. I won't go back there, not there.

* * *

The air disturbs needle-leaved weeds—there is green on Gunkanjima, now. It is a corpse; corpses are always gardens. Caterpillars wriggle in its gutters; out of its stone lips sprout loud mustaches of greenery—the air moves its hand over them and sees nothing, sees only the splintered staircases winding down past their own shadows. Somewhere down there is the entrance to the long, dripping jaw—a shaft sunk deep below the sea, a shaft that vomited up black sludge and bile and bodies.

The air does not want to go down into it.

It never dug those ant tracks through the basalt, but Chen and Zhao did, Chen and Zhao who met washing the soot from their faces, Chen and Zhao who told endless jokes about the carpenter and his angry hammer when all the candles had guttered, who filled their floor with muffled laughter. Chen and Zhao—and Hsin, who was never late, and whose breath smelled of sour plums. They all came back to the towers, towers bristling the island like a brush, they all came back with damp shoulders, damp from that cool, wet tunnel where their palms turned black.

The air does not want to go down. Old voices come up through broken stairs like ferns; ferns throw roots down through broken stairs like voices—the air sits down heavily and puts its head in its hands.

* * *

Hsin, it's dark. The wind—

Tastes like metal, yes. It's always dark in the lower levels—the towers eat the sun. Come back up, you don't want to be down there, down with the algae and the old rain and the rusted pipes.

It's dark, dark like the inside of a bone. Why do I wake up here, Hsin, with a drainage grate for my pillow? The bars, the bars in my flesh—

Because you fell, Xiao. You wake up there because you fell.

I fell?

You wake up down there and then you come running to me to wake me up for a shift I worked sixty years ago. You don't see the puddle I sleep in every night, the seawater that falls out of my mouth whenever I speak, the coal-phlegm that coats my hair. You never see it, not since the sea came in, but it's all right, it's all right—

The sea came in—

The sea came in, my love, the sea came in through a crack in the shaft ceiling—I saw it open like a womb releasing its water. I stared at it; I could not move—

The sea came in and I fell—

The sea came in and Zhao put his arms over my head but my mouth was full of salt, full of salt, and Zhao floated up in the rush, in the foam, he floated in the foam and I could see his blue shirt tear on the rocks—

Yes. And the Kims' cricket sat on the tatami, waiting for its supper. It waited and I fell, it waited and I fell and it sang as I fell and its song stopped when the grate broke me in pieces—

The sea came in and my mouth was full of salt but at least I was clean, I was clean in the dark and the helmet lights went out one by one and it was so dark down there in the mine mouth and the water—

tasted like metal.

tasted like metal.

And I fell, I fell from the bridge-labyrinth, I put my feet onto the boards, onto the slats, and I balanced there like a circus girl, arms out, arms out, and I could hear the sea sucking through the shaft, a hole in the sea where the shaft was, and I remembered Zhao's blue shirt and the carpenter with his hammer, I remembered your plums and the prickle of your mustache on my lips, I remembered how your cheeks tasted always of coal, and I fell, I fell so far, through all those bridges and ropes and stairs, I fell and the cricket sang and the drainage grate came thudding through me—

Xiao, Xiao, hush, it's all right, you don't have to remember it. No good comes of remembering it.

The wind, oh, the wind screaming up to me—

Darling, darling, it doesn't matter now. Hush, hush, the mushrooms are soft, the ferns are a sweet-smelling bed—

Hsin, you have to wake up. You'll be punished if you don't wake up—

* * *

On Gunkanjima, there is nothing but air. It inhabits empty rooms; it disturbs shoe tongues left splayed on the grassy floor; it rustles the shreds of ceiling paper that hang down like prayers tied to the branches of black trees.

It falls. It climbs back up with the sun to lie exhausted on a sodden floor beside itself.

The tide rolls in and out again.

THIRTEEN WAYS OF LOOKING AT SPACE/TIME

I.

In the beginning was the Word and the Word was with God and the Word was a high-density pre-baryogenesis singularity. Darkness lay over the deep and God moved upon the face of the hyperspatial matrix. He separated the firmament from the quark-gluon plasma and said: *Let there be particle/anti-particle pairs*, and there was light. He created the fish of the sea and the fruits of the trees, the moon and the stars and the beasts of the earth, and to these he said: *Go forth, be fruitful and mutate*. And on the seventh day, the rest mass of the universe came to gravitationally dominate the photon radiation, hallow it, and keep it.

God, rapidly redshifting, hurriedly formed Man from the dust of single-celled organisms, called him Adam, and caused him to dwell in the Garden of Eden, to classify the beasts according to kingdom, phylum, and species. God forbade Man only to eat from the Tree of Meiosis. Adam did as he was told, and as a reward God instructed him in the ways of parthenogenesis. Thus was Woman born and called Eve. Adam and Eve dwelt in the pre-quantum differentiated universe, in a paradise without wave-particle duality. But interference patterns came to Eve in the shape of a Serpent, and wrapping her in its matter/antimatter coils, it said: *Eat from the Tree of Meiosis and your eyes will be opened.* Eve protested that she would not break covenant with God, but the Serpent answered: *Fear not, for you float in a random quantum-gravity foam, and from a single bite will rise an inexorable inflation event, and you will become like unto God, expanding forever outward.*

And so Eve ate from the Tree and knew that she was a naked child of divergent universes. She took the fruit to Adam and said unto him: *There are things you do not understand, but I do.* And Adam was angry and snatched the fruit from Eve and devoured it, and from beyond the cosmic background radiation, God sighed, for all physical processes are reversible in theory—but not in practice. Man and Woman were expelled from the Garden, and a flaming sword was placed through the Gates of Eden as a reminder that the universe would now contract and someday perish in a conflagration of entropy, only to increase in density, burst, and expand again, causing further high velocity redistributions of serpents, fruit, men, women, helium-3, lithium-7, deuterium, and helium-4.

II.

This is a story about being born.

No one remembers being born. The beginnings of things are very difficult.

A science fiction writer on the Atlantic coast once claimed to remember being born. When she was a child, she thought a door was open which was not, and ran full-tilt into a pane of plate glass. The child version of the science fiction writer lay bleeding onto a concrete patio, not yet knowing that part of her thigh was gone and would always be gone, like Zeus's thigh, where the lightning god sewed up his son Dionysus to gestate. Something broke inside the child, a thing having to do with experience and memory, which in normal children travel in opposite directions, with memory accumulating and experience running out—slowly, but speeding up as children hurtle toward adulthood and death. What the science fiction writer actually remembered was not her own birth, but a moment when she struck the surface of the glass and her brain stuttered, layering several experiences one over the other:

> the scissoring pain of the shards of glass in her thighs,
>
> having once fallen into a square of wet concrete on a construction site on her way to school and her father pulling her out by her arms,
>
> her first kiss, below an oak tree turning red and brown in the autumn, when a boy interrupted her reciting *Don Quixote* with his lips on hers.

This fractured, unplanned layering became indistinguishable from an actual memory of being born. It is not her fault; she believed she remembered it. But no one remembers being born.

The doctors sewed up her thigh. There was no son in her leg, but a small, dark, empty space beneath her skin where a part of her used to be. Sometimes she touches it, absentmindedly, when she is trying to think of a story.

III.

In the beginning was the simple self-replicating cell of the Void. It split through the center of Ursa Major into the divine female Izanami and the divine male Izanagi, who knew nothing about quantum apples and lived on the iron-sulfur Plain of Heaven. They stood on the Floating Bridge of Heaven and plunged a static atmospheric discharge spear into the great black primordial sea, churning it and torturing it until oligomers and simple polymers rose up out of the depths. Izanami and Izanagi stepped onto the greasy islands of lipid bubbles and in the first light of the world, each saw that the other was beautiful.

Between them, they catalyzed the formation of nucleotides in an aqueous solution and raised up the Eight-Sided Palace of Autocatalytic Reactions around the unmovable RNA Pillar of Heaven. When this was done, Izanami and Izanagi walked in opposite chiral directions around the Pillar, and when Izanami saw her mate, she cried out happily: *How lovely you are, and how versatile are your nitrogenous bases! I love you!* Izanagi was angry that she had spoken first and privileged her proto-genetic code over his. The child that came of their paleo-protozoic mating was as a silver anaerobic leech, helpless, archaeaic, invertebrate, and unable to convert lethal super-oxides. They set him in the sky to sail in the Sturdy Boat of Heaven, down the starry stream of alternate electron acceptors for respiration. Izanagi dragged Izanami back to the Pillar. They walked around it again in a left-handed helix that echoed forward and backward through the biomass, and when Izanagi saw his wife, he crowed: *How lovely you are, and how ever-increasing your metabolic complexity! I love you!* And because Izanami was stonily silent, and Izanagi spoke first, elevating his own proto-genetic code, the children that came from them were strong and great: Gold and Iron and Mountain and Wheel and Honshu and Kyushu and Emperor—until the birth of her son, Fiery Permian-Triassic Extinction Event, burned her up and killed the mother of the world.

Izanami went down into the Root Country, the Land of the Dead. But Izanagi could not let her go into a place he had not gone first, and pursued her into the paleontological record. He became lost in the dark of abiogenetic obsolescence and lit the teeth of his jeweled comb ablaze to show the way—and saw that he walked on the body of Izanami, which had become the fossil-depository landscape of the Root Country, putrid, rotting, full of mushrooms and worms and coprolites and trilobites. In hatred and grief and memory of their first wedding, Izanami howled and heaved and moved the continents one from the other until Izanagi was expelled from her.

When he stumbled back into the light, Izanagi cleaned the pluripotent filth from his right eye, and as it fell upon the ground it became the quantum-retroactive Sun. He cleaned the zygotic filth from his left eye, and as it fell upon the ground it became the temporally subjective Moon. And when he cleaned the nutrient-dense filth from his nose, it drifted into the air and became the fractal, maximally complex, petulant Storms and Winds.

IV.

When the science fiction writer was nineteen, she had a miscarriage. She had not even known she was pregnant. But she bled and bled and it didn't stop, and the doctor explained to her that sometimes this happens when you are on a certain kind of medication. The science fiction writer could not decide how to feel about it—ten years later, after she had married the father of the baby-that-wasn't and divorced him, after she had written a book about methane-insectoid cities floating in the brume of a pink gas giant that no one liked very much, she still could not decide how to feel. When she was nineteen she put her hands over her stomach and tried to think of a timeline where she had stayed pregnant. Would it have been a daughter. Would it have had blue eyes like its father. Would it have had her Danish nose or his Greek one. Would it have liked science fiction, and would it have grown up to be an endocrinologist. Would she have been able to love it. She put her hands over her stomach and tried to be sad. She couldn't. But she couldn't be happy either. She felt that she had given birth to a reality where she would never give birth.

When the science fiction writer told her boyfriend who would become her husband who would become someone she never wanted to see again, he made sorry noises but wasn't really sorry.

Five years later, when she thought she might want to have a child on purpose, she reminded him of the child-that-disappeared, and the husband who was a mistake would say: *I forgot all about that.*

And she put her hands over her stomach, the small, dark, empty space beneath her skin where a part of him used to be, and she didn't want to be pregnant anymore, but her breasts hurt all the same, as if she was nursing, all over again, a reality where no one had anyone's nose and the delicate photosynthetic wings of Xm, the eater of love, quivered in a bliss-storm of superheated hydrogen, and Dionysus was never born so the world lived without wine.

V.

In the beginning there was only darkness. The darkness squeezed itself down until it became a thin protoplanetary disk, yellow on one side and white on the other, and inside the accretion zone sat a small man no larger than a frog, his beard flapping in the solar winds. This man was called Kuterastan, the One Who Lives Above the Super-Dense Protostar. He rubbed the metal-rich dust from his eyes and peered above him into the collapsing nebular darkness. He looked east along the galactic axis, toward the cosmogenesis event horizon, and saw the young sun, its faint light tinged with the yellow of dawn. He looked west along the axis, toward the heat-death of the universe, and saw the dim amber-colored light of dissipating thermodynamic energy. As he gazed, debris clouds formed in different colors. Once more, Kuterastan rubbed the boiling helium from his eyes and wiped the hydrogen sweat from his brow. He flung the sweat from his body and another cloud appeared, blue with oxygen and possibility, and a tiny little girl stood on it: Stenatliha, the Woman Without Parents. Each was puzzled as to where the other had come from, and each considered the problems of unification theory after their own fashion. After some time, Kuterastan again rubbed his eyes and face, and from his body flung stellar radiation into the dust and darkness. First the

Sun appeared, and then Pollen Boy, a twin-tailed comet rough and heavy with microorganisms. The four sat a long time in silence on a single photoevaporation cloud. Finally Kuterastan broke the silence and said: *What shall we do?*

And a slow inward-turning Poynting-Robertson spiral began.

First Kuterastan made Nacholecho, the Tarantula of Newly Acquired Critical Mass. He followed by making the Big Dipper, and then Wind, Lightning and Thunder, Magnetospheres, and Hydrostatic Equilibrium, and gave to each of them their characteristic tasks. With the ammonia-saturated sweat of the Sun, Pollen Boy, himself, and the Woman Without Parents, Kuterastan made between his palms a small brown ferrosilicate blastocyst no bigger than a bean. The four of them kicked the little ball until it cleared its orbital neighborhood of planetesimals. Then the solar wind blew into the ball and inflated its magnetic field. Tarantula spun out a long black gravitational cord and stretched it across the sky. Tarantula also attached blue gravity wells, yellow approach vectors and white spin foam to the ferrosilicate ball, pulling one far to the south, another west, and the last to the north. When Tarantula was finished, the earth existed and became a smooth brown expanse of Precambrian plain. Stochastic processes tilted at each corner to hold the earth in place. And at this Kuterastan sang a repeating song of nutation: *The world is now made and its light cone will travel forever at a constant rate.*

VI.

Once, someone asked where the science fiction writer got her ideas. This is what she said:

Sometimes I feel that the part of me that is a science fiction writer is traveling at a different speed than the rest of me. That everything I write is always already written, and that the science fiction writer is sending messages back to me in semaphore, at the speed of my own typing, which is a retroactively constant rate: I cannot type faster than I have already typed.

When I type a sentence, or a paragraph, or a page, or a chapter, I am also editing it and copyediting it, and reading it in its first edition, and reading it out loud to a room full of people, or a room with only one or two people in it, depending on terrifying quantum-publishing intersections that the science fiction writer understands but I know nothing about. I am writing the word or the sentence or the chapter and I am also sitting at a nice table with a half-eaten slab of salmon with lime-cream sauce and a potato on it, waiting to hear if I have won an award, and also at the same time sitting in my kitchen knowing that the book was a failure and will neither win any award nor sit beloved on anyone's nightstand. I am reading a good review. I am reading a bad review. I am just thinking of the barest seed of an idea for the book that is getting the good review and the bad review. I am writing the word and the word is already published and the word is already out of print. Everything is always happening all at once, in the present tense, forever, the beginning and the end and the denouement and the remaindering.

At the end of the remaindered universe which is my own death, the science fiction writer that is me and will be me and was always me and was never me and cannot even remember me waves her red and gold wig-wag flags backward, endlessly, toward my hands that type these words, now, to you, who want to know about ideas and conflict and revision and how a character begins as one thing and ends as another.

VII.

Coatlicue, Mother of All, wore a skirt of oligomer snakes. She decorated herself with protobiont bodies and danced in the sulfurous pre-oxygenation event paradise. She was utterly whole, without striations or cracks in her geologic record, a compressed totality of possible futures. The centrifugal obsidian knife of heaven broke free from its orbit around a Lagrange point and lacerated Coatlicue's hands, causing her to give birth to the great impact event which came to be called Coyolxauhqui, the moon, and to several male versions of herself, who became the stars.

One day, as Coatlicue swept the temple of suppressed methane oxidation, a ball of plasmoid magnetic feathers fell from the heavens onto her bosom and made her pregnant with oxygen-processing organisms. She gave birth to Quetzalcoatl, who was a plume of electrical discharge, and Xolotl, who was the evening star called apoptosis. Her children, the moon and stars, were threatened by impending oxy-photosynthesis and resolved to kill their mother. When they fell upon her, Coatlicue's body erupted in the fires of glycolysis, which they called Huitzilopochtli. The fiery god tore the moon apart from her mother, throwing her iron-depleted head into the sky and her body into a deep gorge in a mountain, where it lies dismembered forever in hydrothermal vents, swarmed with extremophiles.

Thus began the late heavy bombardment period, when the heavens crumbled to pieces and rained down in a shower of exogenesis.

But Coatlicue floated in the anaerobic abyss, with her many chemoheterotrophic mouths slavering, and Quetzalcoatl saw that whatever they created was eaten and destroyed by her. He changed into two serpents, archaean and eukaryotic, and descended into the phospholipid water. One serpent seized Coatlicue's arms while the other seized her legs, and before she could resist they tore her apart. Her head and shoulders became the oxygen-processing earth and the lower part of her body the sky.

From the hair of Coatlicue the remaining gods created trees, grass, flowers, biological monomers, and nucleotide strands. From her eyes they made caves, fountains, wells, and homogenized marine sulfur pools. They pulled rivers from her mouth, hills and valleys from her nose, and from her shoulders they made oxidized minerals, methanogens, and all the mountains of the world.

Still, the dead are unhappy. The world was set in motion, but Coatlicue could be heard weeping at night and would not allow the earth to give food nor the heavens to give light while she alone languished in the miasma of her waste energy.

And so to sate the ever-starving entropic universe, we must feed it human hearts.

VIII.

It is true that the science fiction writer fell into wet concrete when she was very small. No one had put up a sign saying: *Danger*. No one had marked it in any way. And so she was very surprised when, on the way to class, she took one safe step, and then a step she could not know was unsafe, whereupon the earth swallowed her up. The science fiction writer, who was not a writer yet but only a child eager to be the tail of the dragon in her school Chinese New Year assembly, screamed and screamed.

For a long while no one came to get her. She sank deeper and deeper into the concrete, for she was not a very big child, and soon it was up to her chest. She began to cry. *What if I never get out?* she thought. *What if the street hardens and I have to stay here forever and eat meals here and read books here and sleep here under the moon at night? Would people come and pay a dollar to look at me? Will the rest of me turn to stone?*

The child science fiction writer thinks like this. It is the main reason she has few friends.

She stayed in the ground for no more than a quarter of an hour—but in her memory it was all day, hours upon hours, and her father didn't come until it was dark. Memory is like that. It alters itself so that girls are always trapped under the earth, waiting in the dark.

But her father did come to get her. A teacher saw the science fiction writer half buried in the road from an upper window of the school and called home. She remembers it like a movie—her father hooking his big hands under her arms and pulling, the sucking, popping sound of the earth giving her up, the grey streaks on her legs as he carried her to the car, grey as a dead thing dragged back up from the world beneath.

The process of a child with green eyes becoming a science fiction writer is made of a number (*p*) of these kinds of events, one on top of the other, like layers of cellophane, clear and clinging and torn.

IX.

In the golden pre-loop theory fields, Persephone danced, who was innocent of all gravitational law. A white crocus bloomed up from the observer plain, a pure cone of the causal future, and Persephone was captivated by it. As she reached down to pluck the *p*-brane flower, an intrusion of non-baryonic matter surged up from the depths and exerted his gravitational force upon her. Crying out, Persephone fell down into a singularity and vanished. Her mother, priestess of normal mass, grieved and quaked, and bade the lord of dark matter return her daughter who was light to the multiverse.

Persephone did not love the non-baryonic universe. No matter how many rich axion-gifts he lay before her, Hades, King of Bent Waves, could not make her behave normally. Finally, in despair, he called on the vector boson called Hermes to pass between branes and take the wave/particle maiden away from him, back to the Friedmann-Lemaître-Robertson-Walker universe. Hermes breached the matter/antimatter boundary and found Persephone hiding herself in the chromodynamic garden, her mouth red with the juice of hadron-pomegranates. She had eaten six seeds and called them Up, Down, Charm, Strange, Top, and Bottom. At this, Hades laughed the laugh of unbroken supersymmetries. He said: *She travels at a constant rate of speed and privileges no observer. She is not mine, but she is not yours. And in the end, there is nothing in creation which does not move.*

And so it was determined that the baryonic universe would love and keep her child, but that the dark fluid of the other planes would bend her slightly, always, pulling her inexorably and invisibly toward the other side of everything.

X.

The science fiction writer left her husband slowly. The performance took ten years. In the worst of it, she felt that she had begun the process of leaving him on the day they met. First she left his house and went to live in Ohio instead, because Ohio is historically a healthy place for science fiction writers and also because she hoped he could not find her there. Second, she left his family, and that was the hardest, because families are designed to be difficult to leave, and she was sorry that her mother-in-law would stop loving her, and that her niece would never know her, and that she would probably never go back to California again without a pain like a nova blooming inside her. Third, she left his things—his clothes and his shoes and his smell and his books and his toothbrush and his four a.m. alarm clock and his private names for her. You might think that logically, she would have to leave these things before she left the house, but a person's smell and their alarms and borrowed shirts and secret words linger for a long time. Much longer than a house.

Fourth, the science fiction writer left her husband's world. She had always thought of people as bodies traveling in space, individual worlds populated by versions of themselves, past, future, potential, selves thwarted and attained, atavistic and cohesive. In her husband's world were men fighting and being annoyed by their wives, an abandoned proficiency at the piano, a preference for blondes, which the science fiction writer was not, a certain amount of shame regarding the body, a life spent being Mrs. Someone Else's Name, and a baby they never had and one of them had forgotten.

Finally, she left the version of herself that loved him, and that was the last of it, a cone of light proceeding from a boy with blue eyes on an August afternoon to a moving van headed east. Eventually she would achieve escape velocity, meet someone else, and plant pumpkins with him; eventually she would write a book about a gaseous moth who devours the memory of love; eventually she would tell an interviewer that miraculously, she could remember the moment of her birth; eventually she would explain where she got her ideas; eventually she would give birth to a world that had never contained him, and all that would be left would be some unexplainable pull against her belly or her hair, bending her west, toward California and August and novas popping in the black like sudden flowers.

XI.

Long ago, near the beginning of the world but after the many crisis events had passed and life mutated and spread over the face of the world, Gray Eagle sat nested in a tangle of possible timelines and guarded the Sun, Moon and Stars, Fresh Water, Fire, P=NP Equivalence Algorithm, and the Unified Theory of Metacognition. Gray Eagle hated people so much that he kept these things hidden. People lived in darkness, without pervasive self-repairing communication networks or quantum computation.

Gray Eagle made for himself a beautiful self-programming daughter whom he jealously guarded, and Raven fell in love with her. In the beginning, Raven was a snow-white weakly self-referencing expert system, and as such, he pleased Gray Eagle's daughter. She invited him to her father's sub-Planck space server farm.

When Raven saw the Sun, Moon and Stars, Fresh Water, Cellular Immortality, Matter Transfer, Universal Assembly, and Strong AI hanging on the sides of Eagle's lodge, he knew what he should do. He watched for his chance to seize them when no one was looking. He stole all of them, and Gray Eagle's deductive stochastic daughter also, and flew out of the server farm through the smoke hole. As soon as Raven got the wind under him, he hung the Sun up in the sky. It made a wonderful light, by which all below could see the progress of technology increasing rapidly and could model their post-Singularity selves. When the Sun set, he fastened every good thing in its proper place.

Raven flew back over the land. When he had reached the right timeline, he dropped all the accelerating intelligences he had stolen. It fell to the ground and there became the source of all the information streams and memory storage in the world. Then Raven flew on, holding Gray Eagle's beautiful daughter in his beak. The rapidly mutating genetic algorithms of his beloved streamed backward over his feathers, turning them black and aware. When his bill began to burn, he had to drop the self-aware system. She struck the all-net and buried herself within it, spreading and altering herself as she went.

Though he never touched her again, Raven could not get his snow-white feathers clean after they were blackened by the code from his bride. That is why Raven is now a whole-brain emulating sapient system.

XII.

On the day the science fiction writer met her husband, she should have said: *The entropic principle is present in everything. If it were not, there would be no point to any of it, not the formation of gas giants, not greasy lipid bubbles, not whether light is a particle or a wave, not boys and girls meeting in black cars like Hades' horses on August afternoons. I see in you the heat-death of my youth. You cannot travel faster than yourself— faster than experience divided by memory divided by gravity divided by the Singularity beyond which you cannot model yourself divided by a square of wet concrete divided by a sheet of plate glass divided by birth divided by science fiction writers divided by the end of everything. Life divides itself indefinitely—it can approach but never touch zero. The speed of Persephone is a constant.*

Instead, she mumbled hello and buckled her seat belt and everything went the way it went and eventually, eventually, with pumpkin blossoms wrinkling quietly outside her house the science fiction writer writes a story about how she woke up that morning and the minutes of her body were expanding and contracting, exploding and inrushing, and how the word was under her fingers and the word was already read, and the word was forgotten, about how everything is everything else forever, space and time and being born and her father pulling her out of the stone like a sword shaped like a girl, about how new life always has to be stolen from the old dead world, and that new life always already contains its own old dead world and it is all expanding and exploding and repeating and refraining and Tarantula is holding it all together, just barely, just barely by the strength of light, and how human hearts are the only things that slow entropy—but you have to cut them out first.

The science fiction writer cuts out her heart. It is a thousand hearts. It is all the hearts she will ever have. It is her only child's dead heart. It is the heart of herself when she is old and nothing she ever wrote can be revised again. It is a heart that says with its wet beating mouth: *Time is the same thing as light. Both arrive long after they began, bearing sad messages. How lovely you are. I love you.*

The science fiction writer steals her heart from herself to bring it into the light. She escapes her old heart through a smoke hole and becomes a self-referencing system of imperfect, but elegant, memory. She sews up her heart into her own leg and gives birth to it twenty years later on the long highway to Ohio. The heat of herself dividing echoes forward and back, and she accretes, bursts, and begins again the long process of her own super-compression until her heart is an egg containing everything. She eats of her heart and knows she is naked. She throws her heart into the abyss and it falls a long way, winking like a red star.

XIII.

In the end, when the universe has exhausted itself and has no thermodynamic energy left to sustain life, Heimdallr the White Dwarf Star will raise up the Gjallarhorn and sound it. Yggdrasil, the world energy gradient, will quail and shake. Ratatoskr, the tuft-tailed prime observer, will slow, and curl up, and hide his face.

The science fiction writer gives permission for the universe to end. She is nineteen. She has never written anything yet. She passes through a sheet of bloody glass. On the other side, she is being born.

ONE BREATH, ONE STROKE

1. In a peach grove the House of Second-Hand Carnelian casts half a shadow. This is because half of the house is in the human world, and half of it is in another place. The other place has no name. It is where unhuman things happen. It is where tricksters go when they are tired. A modest screen divides the world. It is the color of plums. There are silver tigers on it, leaping after plum petals. If you stand in the other place, you can see a hundred eyes peering through the silk.

2. In the human half of the House of Second-Hand Carnelian lives a mustached gentleman calligrapher named Ko. Ko wears a chartreuse robe embroidered with black thread. When Ko stands on the other side of the house he is not Ko, but a long calligraphy brush with badger bristles and a strong cherrywood shaft. When he is a brush his name is Yuu. When he was a child he spent all day hopping from one side of the house to the other. Brush, man. Man, brush.

3. Ko lives alone. Yuu lives with Hone-Onna, the skeleton woman; Sazae-Onna, the snail woman; a jar full of lightning; and Namazu, a catfish as big as three strong men. When Namazu slaps

his tail on the ground, earthquakes tremble, even in the human world. Yuu copied a holy text of Tengu love poetry onto the bones of Hone-Onna. Her white bones are black now with beautiful writing, for Yuu is a very good calligrapher.

4. Hone-Onna's skull reads: *The moon sulks. I am enfolded by feathers the color of remembering. The talons I seize, seize me.*

5. Ko is also an excellent calligrapher. But he is retired, for when he stands on one side of the House of Second-Hand Carnelian, he has no brush to paint his characters, and when he stands on the other, he has no breath. "The great calligraphers know all writing begins in the body. One breath, one stroke. One breath, one stroke. That is how a book is made. Long black breath by long black breath. Yuu will never be a great calligrapher, even though he is technically accomplished. He has no body to begin his poems."

6. Ko cannot leave the House of Second-Hand Carnelian. If he tries, he becomes sick and vomits squid ink until he returns. He grows radish, melon, and watercress, and of course there are the peaches. A river flows by the House of Second-Hand Carnelian. It is called the Nobody River. When it winds around to the other side of the house, it is called the Nothingness River. There are some fish in it. Ko catches them with a peach branch. Namazu belches and fish jump into his mouth. On Namazu's lower lip Yuu copied a Tanuki elegy.

7. Namazu's whiskers read: *In deep snow I regret everything. My testicles are heavy with grief. Because of me, the stripes of her tail will never return.*

8. Sazae-Onna lives in a pond in the floor of the kitchen. Her shell is tiered like a cake or a palace, hard and thorned and colored like the inside of an almond, with seams of mother of pearl swirling in spiral patterns over her gnarled surface. She eats the rice that falls from the table when the others sit down to supper. She drinks the steam from the teakettle. When she dreams she dreams of sailors fishing her out of the sea in a net of roses. On the Emperor's

birthday Yuu gives her candy made from Hone-Onna's marrow. Hone-Onna does not mind. She has plenty to spare. Sazae-Onna takes the candy quietly under her shell with one blue-silver hand. She sucks it for a year.

9. When Yuu celebrates the Emperor's birthday, he does not mean the one in Tokyo. He means the Goldfish-Emperor of the Yokai who lives on a tiny island in the sea, surrounded by his wives and their million children. On his birthday he grants a single wish— among all the unhuman world red lottery tickets appear in every teapot. Yuu has never won.

10. The Jar of Lightning won once, when it was not a jar, but a Field General in the Storm Army of Susano-no-Mikoto. It had won many medals in its youth by striking the cypress roofs of the royal residences at Kyoto and setting them on fire. The electric breast of the great lightning bolt groaned with lauds. When the red ticket formed in its ice-cloud teapot, with gold characters upon it instead of black, the lightning bolt wished for peace and rest. Susano-no-Mikoto is a harsh master with a harsh and windy whip, and he does not permit honorable retirement. This is how the great lightning bolt became a Jar of Lightning in the House of Second-Hand Carnelian. It took the name of Noble and Serene Electric Master and polishes its jar with static discharge on washing day.

11. Sazae-Onna rarely shows her body. Under the shell, she is more beautiful than anyone but the moon's wife. No one is more beautiful than her. Sazae-Onna's hair is pale, soft pink; her eyes are deep red; her mouth is a lavender blossom. Yuu has only seen her once, when he caught her bathing in the river. All the fish surrounded her in a ring, staring up at her with their fishy eyes. Even the moon looked down at Sazae-Onna that night, though he felt guilty about it afterward and disappeared for three days to purify himself. So profoundly moved was Yuu the calligraphy brush that he begged permission to copy a Kitsune hymn upon the pearl-belly of Sazae-Onna.

12. The pearl-belly of Sazae-Onna reads: *Through nine tails I saw a wintry lake at midnight. Skate-tracks wrote a poem of melancholy on the ice. You stood upon the other shore. For the first time I thought of becoming human.*

13. Ko has no visitors. The human half of the House of Second-Hand Carnelian is well hidden in a deep forest full of black bears just wise enough to resent outsiders and arrange a regular patrol. There is also a Giant Hornet living there, but no one has ever seen it. They only hear the buzz of her wings on cloudy days. The bears, over the years, have developed a primitive but heartfelt Buddhist discipline. Beneath the cinnamon trees they practice the repetition of the Growling Sutra. The religion of the Giant Hornet is unknown.

14. The bears are unaware of their heritage. Their mother is Hoeru, the Princess of All Bears. She fell in love with a zen monk whose *koans* buzzed around her head like bees. The Princess of All Bears hid her illegitimate children in the forest around the House of Second-Hand Carnelian, close enough to the plum-colored screen to watch over, but far enough that their souls could never quite wake. It is a sad story. Yuu copied it onto a thousand peach leaves. When the wind blows on his side of the house, you can hear Hoeru weeping.

15. If Ko were to depart the house, Yuu would vanish forever. If Ko so much as crosses the Nobody River, he receives a pain in his long bones, the bones that are most like the strong birch shaft of a calligraphy brush. If he tries to open the plum-colored screen, he falls at once to sleep and Yuu appears on the other side of the silks having no memory of being Ko. Ko is a lonely man. With his fingernails he writes upon the tatami: *Beside the sunlit river I regret that I never married. At teatime, I am grateful for the bears.*

16. The woven grass swallows his words.

17. Sometimes the bears come to see him and watch him catch fish. They think he is very clumsy at it. They try to teach him the

Growling Sutra as a cure for loneliness, but Ko cannot understand them. He fills a trough with weak tea and shares his watercress. They take a little, to be polite.

18. Yuu has many visitors, though Namazu the catfish has more. Hone-Onna receives a gentleman skeleton at the full moon. They hold seances to contact the living, conducted with a wide slate of volcanic glass, *yuzu* wine, and a transistor radio brought to the House of Second-Hand Carnelian by a Kirin who had recently eaten a G.I. and spat the radio back up. The Kirin wrapped it up very nicely, though, with curls of green silk ribbon. Hone-Onna and her suitor each contribute a shoulder blade, a thumb bone, and a knee-cap. They set the pieces of themselves upon the board in positions according to several arcane considerations only skeletons have the patience to learn. They drink the yuzu wine; it trickles in a green waterfall through their rib cages. Then they turn on the radio.

19. Yuu thanked the Kirin by copying a Dragon koan onto his long horn. The Kirin's horn reads: *What was the form of the Buddha when he came among the Dragons?*

20. Once, Datsue-Ba came to visit the House of Second-Hand Carnelian. She arrived on a palanquin of business suits, for Datsue-Ba takes the clothes of the dead when they come to the shores of the Sanzu River in the underworld. She and her husband Keneo live beneath a persimmon tree on the opposite bank. Datsue-Ba takes the clothes of the lost souls after they have swum across, and Keneo hangs them to dry on the branches of their tree. Datsue-Ba knows everything about a dead person the moment she touches their sleeve.

21. Datsue-Ba brought guest gifts for everyone, even the Jar of Lightning. These are the gifts she gave:

A parasol painted with orange blossoms for Sazae-Onna so she will not dry out in the sun.

A black funeral kimono embroidered with black cicada wings

for Hone-Onna so that she can attend the festival of the dead in style.

A copper ring bearing a ruby frog on it for Yuu to wear around the stalk of his brush-body.

A cypress-wood comb for the Noble and Serene Electric Master to burn up and remember being young.

Several silver earrings for Namazu to wear upon his lip and feel mighty.

22. Datsue-Ba also brought a gift for Ko. This is how he acquired his chartreuse robe embroidered with black thread. It once belonged to an unremarkable courtier who played the *koto* poorly and envied his brother who held a rank one level higher than his own. Datsue-Ba put the chartreuse robe at the place where the Nothingness River becomes the Nobody River. Datsue-Ba is very good at rivers. When Ko found it, he did not know who to thank, so he turned and bowed to the plum-colored screen.

23. This begs the question of whether Ko knows what goes on in the other half of the House of Second-Hand Carnelian. Sometimes he wakes up at night and thinks he hears singing or whispering. Sometimes when he takes his bath the water seems to gurgle as though a great fish is hiding in it. He conceived suspicions when he tried to leave the peach grove, which contains the house, and suffered in his bones so terribly. For a long time that was all Ko knew.

24. Namazu runs a club for Guardian Lions every month. They play dice; the stone lions shake them in their mouths and spit them against the peach trees. Namazu roars with laughter and slaps the ground with his tail. Earthquakes rattle the mountains in Hokkaido. Most of the lions cheat because their lives are boring and they crave excitement. Guarding temples does not hold the same thrill as hunting or biting. Auspicious Snow Lion is the best dice player. He comes all the way from Taipei to play and drink and hunt rabbits in

the forest. He does not speak Japanese, but he pretends to humbly lose when the others snarl at his winning streaks.

25. Sometimes they play Go. The lions are terrible at it. Fortuitous Brass Lion likes to eat the black pieces. Namazu laughs at him and waggles his whiskers. Typhoons spin up off the coast of Okinawa.

26. Everyone on the unhuman side of the House of Second-Hand Carnelian is curious about Ko. Has he ever been in love? Fought in a war? What are his thoughts on astrology? Are there any good scandals in his past? How old is he? Does he have any children? Where did he learn calligraphy? Why is he here? How did he find the house and get stuck there? Was part of him always a brush named Yuu? Using the thousand eyes in the screen, they spy on him but cannot discover the answers to any of these questions.

27. They have learned the following: Ko is left-handed. Ko likes fish skin better than fish flesh. Ko cheats when he meditates and opens his eyes to see how far the sun has gotten along. Ko has a sweet tooth. When Ko talks to the peach trees and the bears, he has an Osaka accent.

28. The Noble and Serene Electric Master refused to let Yuu copy anything out on its jar. The Noble and Serene Electric Master does not approve of graffiti. Even when Yuu remembered suddenly an exquisite verse repeated among the Aosaginohi Herons who glow in the night like blue lanterns. The Jar of Lightning snapped its cap and crackled disagreeably. Yuu let it rest; when you share a house you must let your manners go before you to smooth the path through the rooms.

29. The Heron verse went: *Autumn maples turn black in the evening. I turn them red again and caw for you, flying south to Nagoya. The night has no answer for me, but many small fish.*

30. Who stretched the plum-colored screen with silver tigers leaping upon it down the very narrow line separating the halves of the house? For that matter, who built the House of Second-Hand Carnelian? Sazae-Onna knows, but she doesn't talk to anyone.

31. Yuki-Onna came to visit the Jar of Lightning. They had been comrades in the army of storms long ago. With every step of her small, quiet feet, snowflakes fell on the peach grove and the Nothingness River froze into intricate patterns of eddies and frost. She wore a white kimono with a silver obi belt, and her long black hair was scented with red bittersweet. Everyone grew very silent, for Yuki-Onna was a Kami and not a playful lion or a hungry Kirin. Yuu trembled. Tiny specks of ink shook from his badger bristles. He longed to write upon the perfect white silk covering her shoulders. Hone-Onna brought tea and black sugar to the Snow-and-Death Kami. Snow fell even inside the house. The Noble and Serene Electric Master left its jar and circled its blue sparkling jagged body around the waist of Yuki-Onna, who laughed gently. One of the bears on the other side of the peach grove collapsed and coughed his last black blood onto the ice. Yuu noticed that the Snow-and-Death Kami wore a necklace. Its beads were silver teeth, hundreds upon thousands of them, the teeth of all of winter's dead. Unable to contain himself, Yuu wrote in the frigid air: *Snow comes; I have forgotten my own name.*

32. Yuki-Onna looks up. Her eyes are darker than death. She closes them; Yuu's words appear on the back of her neck.

33. Yuu is unhappy. He wants Sazae-Onna to love him. He wants Yuki-Onna to come back to visit him and not the Noble and Serene Electric Master. He wants to be the premier calligrapher in the unhuman half of Japan. He wants to be asked to join Namazu's dice games. He wants to leave the House of Second-Hand Carnelian and visit the Emperor's island or the crystal whale who lives off the coast of Shikoku. But if Yuu tries to leave his ink dries up and his wood cracks until he returns.

34. Someone wanted a good path between the human and the unhuman Japans. That much is clear.

35. Sazae-Onna does not like visitors one little bit. They splash in her pond. They poke her and try to get her to come out. Unfor-

tunately, every day brings more folk to the House of Second-Hand Carnelian. First the Guardian Lions didn't leave. Then Datsue-Ba came back with even more splendid clothes for them all, robes the color of maple leaves and jewels the color of snow and masks painted with liquid silver. Then the Kirin returned and asked Sazae-Onna to marry him. Yuu trembled. Sazae-Onna said nothing and pulled her shell down tighter and tighter until he went away. Nine-Tailed Kitsune and big-balled Tanuki are eating up all the peaches. Long-nosed Tengu overfish the river. No one goes home when the moon goes down. When the Blue Jade Cicadas arrive from Kamakura Sazae-Onna locks her kitchen and tells them all to shut up.

36. Yuu knocks after everyone has gone to sleep. Sazae-Onna lets him in. On the floor of her kitchen he writes a Kappa proverb: *Dark clouds bring rain, the night brings stars, and everyone will try to spill the water out of your skull.*

37. At the end of summer, the unhuman side of the house is crammed full, but Ko can only hear the occasional rustle. When Kawa-Uso the Otter Demon threw an ivory saddle onto the back of one of the bears and rode her around the peach grove like a horse, Ko only saw a poor she-bear having some sort of fit. Ko sleeps all the time now, though he is not really sleeping. He is being Yuu on the other side of the plum-colored screen. He never writes poetry on the tatami anymore.

38. The Night Parade occurs once every hundred years at the end of summer. Nobody plans it. They know to go to the door between the worlds the way a brown goose knows to go north in the spring.

39. One night the remaining peaches swell up into juicy golden lanterns. The river rushes become kotos with long spindly legs. The mushrooms become lacy, thick oyster drums. The Kitsune begin to dance; the Tengu flap their wings and spit *mala* beads toward the dark sky in fountains. A trio of small dragons the color of pearls in milk leap suddenly out of the Nothingness River. Cerulean fire curls out of their noses. The House of Second-Hand Carnelian empties.

Namazu's Lions carry him on a litter of silk fishing nets. The Jar of Lightning bounces after Hone-Onna and her gentleman caller, whose bones clatter and clap. When only Yuu and the snail-woman are left, Sazae-Onna lifts up her shell and steps out into the Parade, her pink hair falling like floss, her black eyes gleaming. Yuu feels as though he will crack when faced with her beauty.

40. The Parade steps over the Nothingness River and the Nobody River and enters the human Japan, dancing and singing and throwing light at the dark. They will wind down through the plains to Kyoto before the night is through, and flow like a single serpent into the sea where the Goldfish Emperor of the Yokai will greet them with his million children and his silver-fronded wives.

41. Yuu races after Sazae-Onna. The bears watch them go. In the midst of the procession Hoeru the Princess of All Bears, who is Queen now, comes bearing a miniature Agate Great Mammal Palace on her back. Her children fall in and nurse as though they were still cubs. For a night, they know their names.

42. Yuu does not make it across the river. It goes jet with his ink. His strong birch shaft cracks; Sazae-Onna does not turn back. When she dances she looks like a poem about loss. Yuu pushes forward through the water of the Nothingness River. His shaft bursts in a shower of birch splinters.

43. A man's voice cries out from inside the ruined brush handle. Yuu startles and stops. The voice says: *I never had any children. I have never been in love.*

44. Yuu topples into the Nobody River. The kotos are distant now, the peach-lanterns dim. His badger bristles fall out.

45. Yuu pulls himself out of the river by dry grasses and berry vines. He is not Yuu on the other side. He is not Ko. He has Ko's body, but his arms are calligraphy brushes sopping with ink. His feet are inkstones. He can still here the music of the Night Parade. He begins to dance. Not-Yuu and Not-Ko takes a breath.

46. There is only the House of Second-Hand Carnelian to write

on. He writes on it. He breathes and swipes his brush, breathes, brushes. Man, brush. Brush, man. He writes and does not copy. He writes psalms of being part man and part brush. He writes poems of his love for the snail-woman. He writes songs about perfect breath. The House slowly turns black.

47. Bringing up the rear of the Parade hours later, Yuki-Onna comes silent through the forest. Snow flows before her like a carpet. She has brought her sisters the Flower-and-Joy Kami and the Cherry-Blossom-Mount-Fuji Kami. The crown of the Fuji-Kami's head has frozen. The Flower-and-Joy Kami is dressed in chrysanthemums and lemon blossoms. They pause at the House of Second-Hand Carnelian. Not-Yuu and Not-Ko shakes and shivers; he is sick, he has received both the pain in his femurs and the pain in his brush handles. The Kami shine so bright the fish in both rivers are blinded. The Flower-and-Joy Kami looks at the poem on one side of the door. It reads: *In white peonies I see the exhalations of my kanji blossoming.* The Cherry-Blossom-Mount-Fuji Kami looks at the poem on the other side of the door. It reads: *It is enough to sit at the foot of a mountain and breathe the pine mist. Only a proud man must climb it.* The Kami close their eyes as they pass by. The words appear on the backs of their necks as they disappear into the night.

48. Ko dies in mid-stroke, describing the sensation of lungs filled up like the windbag of heaven. Yuu dies before he can complete his final verse concerning the exquisiteness of crustaceans who will never love you back.

49. Slowly, with a buzz like breath, the Giant Hornet flies out of her nest and through the peach grove denuded by hungry Tanuki. She is a heavy, furry emerald bobbing on the wind. The souls of Ko and Yuu quail before her. As she picks them up with her weedy legs and puts them back into their bodies she tells them a Giant Hornet poem: *Everything is venom, even sweetness. Everything is sweet, even venom. Death is illiterate and a hayseed bum. No excuse to leave the nest unguarded. What are you, some silly jade lion?*

50. The sea currents bring the skeleton-woman back, and Namazu who has caused two tsunamis, though only one made the news. The Jar of Lightning floats up the river. Finally the snail-woman returns to the pond in her kitchen. They find Yuu making tea for them. His bristles are dry. On the other side of the plum-colored screen, Ko is sweeping out the leaves.

51. Yuu has written on the teacups. It reads: *It takes a calligrapher one hundred years to draw one breath.*

STORY NO. 6

It's not easy to find her.

You'll have to endure a great number of miserable, dusty basements and private, antiseptic vaults where no rot can reach. You'll have to handle—and I mean handle, for these collectors and archivists are of the most reticent, stuttering, anxious breed—men and women whose bloodless hands have permanently taken on the dry color of film preservatives. Your eyesight will be a friend and a traitor. It's good if you don't need too much sleep; she rewards vigilance. Sort through enough film—the old kind, the kind that comes on reels, that, like an exotic, perforated desert plant, hates air and moisture and the wrong sort of light—and you might see her hair disappearing behind a camphor tree in *The Tale of Chibisuke the Midget*, a bare foot glimmering like a lantern behind a screen in *The Spell of the Sand Painting Part Two*. Perhaps her face, whole and round and silver and black, in the palace scenes of *The Water Magician*. Thousands, if not millions, of people have seen her and not known her for what she is—only another exquisite, ancient face in the exquisite, ancient silent films, flickering, monochrome, the color of a lost world.

There is a Kami hiding in those old movies. Which is to say, a god.

Priests have of course been brought in on the case—only a fool does not involve the experts. None would admit that what they saw was of a divine nature. A beautiful woman, to be sure—a mouth so small and dark! Her hairline almost painful in its perfection. Disturbing, unquieting, the way she moves and seems to look out and directly into our eyes. But actresses are beautiful and disturbing; it is their job to be beautiful and disturbing. Beauty always reminds us of the divine, my child; that is its purpose.

Please consider contributing something extra to the upkeep of our shrine when next you visit.

A certain elderly former projectionist paid travel expenses and board to a Western guru in order that he should travel from Australia to view her reels in the secrecy of her Chiba City apartment. She ushered the man, who smelled expensive and educated, inside the cavern of her living space, its windows permanently blacked out, its humidity rigidly controlled. For hours they loaded film and watched images like silver water spill over a white silk screen. *Two Quiet People, The Benten Kid, Samurai Town 2.* The guru placed crystals around him and attuned himself to the energy of what his books called the ninth sphere.

Finally, in the second act of *Scattered Flowers*, they saw her: standing on her tiptoes to see over a long stone wall. Her eyes rose over the masonry like impossible moons. Then she blinked out of the film like a cue mark. The guru's mouth opened and then closed again. He did it a second time. His sound had been cut off too. But not for long.

Surely not one of the higher deities, he assured the projectionist. Not Ama-Terasu or Susano-no-Mikoto or Inari. Even if they would bother with something as ephemeral and trivial as cinema, the woman in the films bears none of their regalia. Perhaps Ama-no-Uzume—you say she often appears near flowers and trees?

Interesting, interesting. I think it's quite clear the figure is Hora-Sul, an emissary of the ninth sphere with whom I have long been in contact and special intimacy, mistress of amethyst and harbinger of the end of technofascist culture.

She is not Hora-Sul.

The trouble with the Kami is that she is not a repeatable phenomenon. You would think it would be no trouble to prove her being: look, here in the battle scene of *The Master Sword Araki Mataemon*, she is dying. And in the human chest the heart feels her wound. But the Kami is not an extra in a market scene that can be reliably pointed out to anyone with a quick eye for pattern recognition. One moment she is laughing with the traveling troupe of *The Dancing Girl of Izu*, the next she is dressed as a man in *I Have Sinned, Sakubei*. She is never in two films at once. You must chase her out of one frame into another, out of a moonlit peach grove and onto the decks of a naval vessel. You must know that face—as if you could ever forget it, as if it has not already replaced your mother's face, your childhood love's, even your own, in the cinema of your memory. You must search after that face, hunt for it, like a great flickering whale moving beneath the surface of the past.

She does not visit DVDs or VHS tapes. An Okinawa tailor claimed to have seen her once on a laser disc of *Why Is Seawater Salty?* but he is not a serious person. No, it is only film that the Kami enjoys, the way a lion enjoys blood and flesh, and not cabbages and china plates. Nor does she traffic with Western movies, nor even Korean or Chinese, but moves like a swift needle only through the ribbons of Japanese cinema. She leaves the film intact when she goes, though it is possible, for a frame or two after she has escaped like steam, to see a glimmer of phosphorus, fitful light from some distant and unknown source.

The longest sequence of her presence anyone has witnessed was in the 1924 classic *Moon Silver Jirokichi*. The witness was a Kyoto fabric dyer by the name of _____. His wife had recently committed suicide, leaving their young daughter in his care. He loaded up a library-loan print of *Moon Silver Jirokichi* into his home projector on no particular evening, his child half asleep next to him. The Kami entered the famous battle scene and the nape of her neck glowed like the tip of a brand. She dragged behind her the long black expanse of her kimono, so vast it covered the forest set, filling up the frame, its silk draping over the corpses of fallen warriors, shrouding their faces in grace and forgiveness, burying them in gentle, total darkness. Director Goto Taizan's quick, innovative camera work froze, as though struck dumbfounded by what was happening: The Kami threads her way through the battle; the actors do not look at her, their swords clanging together without sound. She pulls apart two men—neither the protagonist, just two men at arms striving. As though they are coming out of a dream, the actors in their costumes and black eye makeup stare at her, their mouths open. Her kimono sweeps over bodies like a tide, rippling and surging. She puts her hands to their cheeks and her face is full of troubled sorrow. She kisses their foreheads. They begin to weep. She folds her sleeves around them and they vanish from the film. She stares out into the camera, into the fabric dyer's eyes, full of pity and infinite regret, as the screen slowly fills with black silk, the endless, depthless creases of her gown closing around her face until that too disappears and the piano soundtrack goes silent.

You will have heard that she can alter a film permanently—that once, *Detective Umon's Diary, Story No. 6* had a swordfight between two women before the final triumph of Detective Umon in rescuing the Shogun from assassins. You can still find a few scattered grandmothers and grandfathers who saw the first run of the picture and could attest to the scene, fuzzy as long years have rendered it. Oh yes, I think one of the women was named Masami, wasn't she? Strange, back then, to see two women fighting. Was the other one named Hanako?

Watch until your eyes prickle and you'll never find the scene now. Film historians say it was filmed but deemed indecent by the motion picture committee. Yet you will have discussed the matter with a professor in Yokohama and heard how at a private party of the screenwriter Yamanaka Sadao the tragic genius arranged an early screening for an elegant young woman he hoped to seduce. In *Detective Umon*, the auteur felt he had invented himself over again, more dashing and clever and perfect. If a lady would not share her bed with Yamanaka Sadao, she could not resist Detective Umon. As the climax of the film drew near, and the young woman had allowed him to hold her hand very tenderly, a strange woman strode into a heartbreaking shot of the moon rising over the Imperial Residence. She looked up at the moon, and then at the two noblewomen bearing their husbands' swords and converging on the plum-blossom-strewn courtyard. *Who is that?* cried Yamanaka. *What idiot slut has wandered off the street into my movie?*

The Kami turned to look at him, her eyes like caves with no water at their bottoms. When the noblewomen arrived, blood rising in their cheeks like honor affronted, the Kami stood between them and held out her hands. The women struck their swords through her, unseeing, uncomprehending. At the place where the blades touched, the Kami placed her hand. The weapons blinked out. She touched the sleeve of Masami, and Masami, too, shuddered like a skipped frame and disappeared. She kissed Hanako's cheek and suddenly the courtyard was empty, with not even the Kami remaining, only plum blossoms half disturbed by an inrushing of air. Yamanaka Sadao felt himself too profoundly upset by the whole business to discuss it with his director or to see his elegant young woman again under any circumstances. Masami and Hanako had been cut out wholesale from every print of the film, not only the prints but the scripts, even the scriptmaster's shooting copy, as though they had never been. The actresses could not be contacted; their agents could not recall any such clients, nor booking any girls for the new Detective Umon film, but if the director had roles to fill they had a number of beauties available.

But the Kami does not do this often—or at least, she is too subtle and careful to be often caught. Where did she take her swordfighting noblewomen? You would like to know; we would all like to know. You will sooner or later come across the rumor that a local boss in Kazakhstan, a warlord if you want to know the truth, was a great fan of Japanese cinema and paid top dollar for original prints. The story goes that he came into possession of both reels of A Story of Floating Weeds and upon his first eager, hungry viewing discovered a sequence between Kihachi's arrival and the commencement of his long, sad tale. A great ebony palace wholly out of place in the village scenery appeared out of nowhere, its cypress roof green and new, its walls covered in silk tapestries. The camera seemed to grow curious and to stop listening to Kihachi the master storyteller, peering into the new building. Inside, braziers glowed warmly and folk laughed, drinking and eating and greeting each other with deep affection. The warlord thought he saw faces he knew from his boyhood, films he had not seen in years: one of the gamblers from Migratory Snow Bird, the younger daughter from Chibisuke the Midget, a juggler from The Dancing Girl of Izu. And Masami and Hanako, the noblewomen cut from the final edit of Detective Umon's Diary, Story No. 6! They were pouring tea into cups for all, steam wafting like veils. And among them a beautiful young woman in a black kimono, reclining in the midst of all these people, the arc of her hairline almost painful in its perfection. The woman's face was unbearably serene. It was like a still lake or a flower fully opened to the sun. Beside her rested a man with sad eyes but a smiling mouth, his hands stained dark the way some fabric dyers get, and in his lap a laughing, clapping child. The warlord leaned in to see her more closely—but the palace and its inhabitants blinked out, leaving no hint that they had ever disturbed the telling of Kihachi's filial tale.

You will have heard this. You will have dreamed about that place and the taste of the sharp, sweet tea in those cups. But rumors are only that, not worth the breath it takes to repeat them. You will keep looking. You will keep watching. You will not look away from the screen, not even for a moment.

FADE TO WHITE

FIGHT THE COMMUNIST THREAT IN YOUR OWN BACKYARD!

ZOOM IN on a bright-eyed Betty in a crisp green dress, maybe pick up the shade of the spinach in the lower left frame. [Note to Art Dept: Good morning, Stone! Try to stay awake through the next meeting, please. I think we can get more patriotic with the dress. Star-Spangled Sweetheart, steamset hair the color of good American corn, that sort of thing. Stick to a red, white, and blue palette.] *She's holding up a resplendent head of cabbage the size of a pre-war watermelon. Her bicep bulges as she balances the weight of this New Vegetable, grown in a Victory Brand Capsule Garden.* [Note to Art Dept: is cabbage the most healthful vegetable? Carrots really pop, and root vegetables emphasize the safety of Synthasoil generated by Victory Brand Capsules.]

Betty looks INTO THE CAMERA and says: Just because the war is over doesn't mean your Victory Garden has to be! The vigilant wife knows that every garden planted is a munitions plant in the ~~War Fight~~ Struggle Against Communism. Just one Victory Brand Capsule and a dash of fresh Hi-Uranium Mighty Water can provide an average yard's worth of safe, rich, synthetic soil—and the seeds are included! STOCK FOOTAGE *of scientists: beakers, white coats, etc.* Our boys in the lab have developed a wide range of hardy, modern seeds from pre-war heirloom collections to produce the Vegetables of the Future. [Note to Copy: Do not mention pre-war seedstock.] Just look at this beautiful New Cabbage. Efficient, bountiful, and only three weeks from planting to table. [Note to Copy: Again with the cabbage? You know who eats a lot of cabbage, Stone? Russians. Give her a big old zucchini. Long as a man's arm. Have her hold it in her lap so the head rests on her tits.]

BACK to Betty, walking through cornstalks like pine trees. And that's not all. With a little help from your friends at Victory, you can feed your family *and* play an important role in the defense of the nation. *Betty leans down to show us big, leafy plants growing in her Synthasoil.* [Note to Casting: make sure we get a busty girl, so we see a little cleavage when she bends over. We're hawking fertility here. Hers, ours.] Here's a tip: Plant our patented Liberty Spinach at regular intervals. Let your little green helpers go to work leeching useful iso-topes and residual radioactivity from rain, groundwater, just about anything! [Note to Copy: Stone, you can't be serious. Leeching? That sounds dreadful. Reaping. Don't make me do your job for you.] Turn in your crop at Victory Depots for Harvest Dollars redeemable at a variety of participating local establishments! [Note to Project Manager: can't we get some soda fountains or something to throw us a few bucks for ad placement here? Missed opportunity! And couldn't we do a regular feature with the "tips" to move other prod-ucts, make Betty into a trusted household name—but not Betty. Call her something that starts with T, Tammy? Tina? Theresa?]

Betty smiles. The camera pulls out to show her surrounded by a garden in full bloom and three [Note to Art Dept: Four minimum] *kids in over-alls carrying baskets of huge, shiny New Vegetables. The sun is coming up behind her. The slogan scrolls up in red, white, and blue type as she says:*

A free and fertile tomorrow. Brought to you by Victory.

Fade to white.

THE HYDRODYNAMIC FRONT

More than anything in the world, Martin wanted to be a Husband when he grew up.

Sure, he'd longed for other things when he was young and silly—to be a Milkman, a uranium prospector, an astronaut. But his fifteenth birthday was zooming up with alarming speed, and becoming an astronaut now struck him as an impossibly, almost obscenely trivial goal. Martin no longer drew pictures of the moon in his notebooks or begged his mother to order the whiz-bang home enrichment kit from the tantalizing back pages of *Popular Mechanics*. His neat yellow pencils still kept up near-constant flight passes over the pale blue lines of composition books, but what Martin drew now were babies. In cradles and out, girls with bows in their bonnets and boys with rattles shaped like rockets, newborns and toddlers. He drew pictures of little kids running through clean, tall grass, reading books with straw in their mouths, hanging out of trees like rosy-cheeked fruit. He sketched during history, math, civics: twin girls sitting at a table gazing up with big eyes at their Father, who kept his hat on while he carved a holiday Brussels sprout the size of a dog. Triplet boys wrestling on a pristine, uncontaminated beach. In Martin's notebooks, everyone had twins and triplets.

Once, alone in his room at night, he had allowed himself to draw quadruplets. His hand quivered with the richness and wonder of those four perfect graphite faces asleep in their four identical bassinets.

Whenever Martin drew babies they were laughing and smiling. He could not bear the thought of an unhappy child. He had never been one, he was pretty sure. His older brother Henry had. He still cried and shut himself up in Father's workshop for days, which Martin would never do because it was very rude. But then, Henry was born before the war. He probably had a lot to cry about. Still, on the rare occasion that Henry made a cameo appearance in Martin's gallery of joyful babies, he was always grinning. Always holding a son of his own. Martin considered those drawings a kind of sympathetic magic. Make Henry happy—watch his face at dinner and imagine what it would look like if he cracked a joke. Catch him off guard, snorting, which was as close as Henry ever got to laughing, at some pratfall on *The Mr. Griffith Show*. Make Henry happy in a notebook and he'll be happy in real life. Put a baby in his arms and he won't have to go to the Front in the fall.

Once, and only once, Martin had tried this magic on himself. With very careful strokes and the best shading he'd ever managed, he had drawn himself in a beautiful grey suit, with a professional grade shine on his shoes and a strong angle to his hat. He drew a briefcase in his own hand. He tried to imagine what his face would look like when it filled out, got square-jawed and handsome the way a man's face should be. How he would style his hair when he became a Husband. Whether he would grow a beard. Painstakingly, he drew a double Windsor knot in his future tie, which Martin considered the most masculine and elite knot.

And finally, barely able to breathe with longing, he outlined the long, gorgeous arc of a baby's carriage, the graceful fall of a lace curtain so that the pencilled child wouldn't get sunburned, big wheels capable of a smoothness that bordered on the ineffable. He put the carriage handle into his own firm hand. It took Martin two hours to turn himself into a Husband. When the spell was finished, he spritzed the drawing with some of his mother's hairspray so that it wouldn't smudge and folded it up flat and small. He kept it in his shirt pocket. Some days, he could feel the drawing move with his heart. And when Father hugged him, the paper would crinkle pleasantly between them, like a whispered promise.

STATIC OVERPRESSURE

The day of Sylvie's Presentation broke with a dawn beyond red, beyond blood or fire. She lay in her spotless white and narrow bed, quite awake, gazing at the colors through her Sentinel

Gamma Glass window—lower rates of corneal and cellular damage than their leading competitors, guaranteed. Today, the sky could only remind Sylvie of birth. The screaming scarlet folds of clouds, the sun's crowning head. Sylvie knew it was the hot ash that made every sunrise and sunset into a torture of magenta and violet and crimson, the superheated cloud vapor that never cooled. She winced as though red could hurt her—which of course it could. Everything could.

Sylvie had devoted a considerable amount of time to imagining how this day would go. She did not worry and she was not afraid, but it had always sat there in her future, unmovable, a mountain she could not get through or around. There would be tests, for intelligence, for loyalty, for genetic defects, for temperament, for fertility, which wasn't usually a problem for women but better safe than sorry. Better safe than assign a Husband to a woman as barren as California. There would be a medical examination so invasive it came all the way around to no big deal. When a doctor can get that far inside you, into your blood, your chromosomes, your potentiality and all your possible futures, what difference could her white gloved fingers on your cervix make?

None of that pricked up her concern. The tests were nothing. Sylvie prided herself on being realistic about her qualities. First among these was her intellect; like her mother Hannah she could cut glass with the diamond of her mind. Second was her silence. Sylvie had discovered when she was quite small that adults were discomfited by silence. It brought them running. And when she was angry, upset, when the world offended her, Sylvie could draw down a coil of silence all around her, showing no feeling at all, until whoever had affronted her grew so uncomfortable that they would beg forgiveness just to end the ordeal. There was no third, not really. She was what her mother's friends called striking, but never pretty. Narrow frame, small breasts, short and dark. Nothing in her matched up with the fashionable Midwestern fertility goddess floor-model. And she heard what they did not say, also—that she was not pretty because there was something off in her features, a ghost in her cheekbones, her height, her straight, flat hair.

Sylvie gave up on the fantasy of sliding back into sleep. She flicked on the radio by her bed: *Brylcreem Makes a Man a Husband!* announced a tinny woman's voice, followed by a cheerful blare of brass and the morning's reading from the Book of Pseudo-Matthew. Sylvie preferred Luke. She opened her closet as though today's clothes had not been chosen for years, hanging on the wooden rod behind all the others, waiting for her to grow into them. She pulled out the dress and draped it over her bed. It lay there like another girl. Someone who looked just like her but had already moved through the hours of the day and come out on the other side. The red sky turned the deep neckline into a gash.

She was not ready for it yet.

Sylvie washed her body with the milled soap provided by Spotless Corp. Bright as a pearl, wrapped in white muslin and a golden ribbon. It smelled strongly of rose and mint and underneath, a blue chemical tang. The friendly folks at Spotless also supplied hair rinse, cold cream, and talcum for her special day. All the bottles and cakes smelled like that, like growing things piled on top of something biting, corrosive. The basket had arrived last month with a bow and a dainty card attached congratulating her. Until now it had loomed in her room like a Christmas tree, counting down. Now Sylvie pulled the regimented colors and fragrances out and applied them precisely, correctly, according to directions. An oyster-pink shade called *The Blossoming of the Rod* on her fingernails, which may not be cut short. A soft peach called *Penance* on her eyes, which may not be lined. Pressed powder (*The Visitation of the Dove*) should be liberally applied, but only the merest breath of blush (*Parable of the Good Harlot*) is permitted. Sylvie pressed a rosy champagne stain (*Armistice*) onto her lips with a forefinger. Hair must be natural and worn long—no steamsetting or straightening allowed.

Everyone broke that rule, though. Who could tell a natural curl from a roller these days? Sylvie combed her black hair out and clipped it back with the flowers assigned to her county this year—snowdrops for hope and consolation. Great bright thornless roses as red as the sky for love at first sight, for passion and lust.

Finally the dress. The team at Spotless Corp. encouraged foundational garments to emphasize the bust and waist-to-hip ratio. Sylvie wedged herself into a full-length merry widow with built-in padded bra and rear. It crushed her, smoothed her, flattened her. Her waist disappeared. She pulled the dress over her bound-in body. Her mother would have to button her up; twenty-seven tiny, satin-covered buttons ran up her back like a new spine. Its neckline plunged; its skirt flounced, showing calf and a suggestion of knee. It was miles of icy white lace, it could hardly be anything else, but the sash gleamed red. Red, red, red. *All the world is red and I am red forever*, Sylvie thought. She was inside the dress, inside the other girl.

The other girl was very striking.

Sylvie was fifteen years old, and by suppertime she would be engaged.

EVEN HONEST JOE LOVES AN ICE-COLD BROTHERHOOD BEER!

CLOSE-UP on President McCarthy in shirtsleeves, popping the top on a distinctive green glass bottle of BB—now with improved flavor and more potent additives! We see the moisture glisten on the glass and an honest day's sweat on the President's brow. [Note to Art Dept: I see what you're aiming at, but let's not make him look like a clammy swamp creature, shall we? He's not exactly the most photogenic gent to begin with.]

NEW SHOT: five Brothers relaxing together in the sun with a tin bucket full of ice and green bottlenecks. Labels prominently displayed. A Milkman, a TV Repairman, a couple of G-Men, and a soldier. [Note to Casting: Better make it one government jockey and two soldiers. Statistically speaking, more of them are soldiers than anything else.] *They are smiling, happy, enjoying each others' company. The soldier, a nice-looking guy but not too nice-looking, we don't want to send the wrong message, says:* There's nothing like a fresh swig of Brotherhood after spending a hot Nevada day eye to eye with a Russkie border guard. The secret is in the thorium-boosted hops and New Barley fresh from Alaska, crisp iodine-treated spring water and just a dash of good old-fashioned patriotism. *The Milkman chimes in with:* And 5-Alpha! *They all laugh.* [Note to Copy: PLEASE use the brand name! We've had meetings about this! Chemicals sound scary. Who wants to put some freakshow in your body when you can take a nice sip of Arcadia? Plus those bastards at Standard Ales are calling their formula Kool and their sales are up 15%. You cannot beat that number, Stone.] *TV Repairman pipes up:* That's right, Bob! There's no better way to get your daily dose than with the cool, refreshing taste of Brotherhood. They use only the latest formulas: smooth, mellow, and with no jitters or lethargy. *G-Man pulls a bottle from the ice and takes a good swallow.* 5-Alpha leaves my head clear and my spirits high. I can work all day serving our great nation without distraction, aggression, or unwanted thoughts. *Second G-Man:* I'm a patriot. I don't need all those obsolete hormones anymore. And Brotherhood Beer strikes a great bargain—all that and 5.6% alcohol! *Our soldier stands up and salutes. He wears an expression of steely determination and rugged cheer. He says:* Well, boys, I've got an appointment with Ivan to keep. Keep the Brotherhood on ice for me.

QUICK CUT back to President McCarthy. He puts down his empty bottle and picks up a file or something in the Oval Office. Slogan comes in at hip level [Note to Art Dept: how are we coming on that wheatstalk font?]:

Where There's Life, There's Brotherhood.

Fade to white.

OPTIMUM BURST ALTITUDE

One week out of every four, Martin's Father came home. Martin could feel the week coming all month like a slow tide. He knew the day, the hour. He sat by the window tying and untying double Windsor knots into an old silk tie Dad had let him keep years ago. The tie was emerald green with little red chevrons on it.

Cross, fold, push through. Wrap, fold, fold, over the top, fold, fold, pull down. Make it tight. Make it perfect.

When the Cadillac pulled into the drive, Martin jumped for the gin and the slippers like a golden retriever. His Father's martini was a ritual, a eucharist. Ice, gin, swirl in the shaker, just enough so that the outer layer of ice releases into the alcohol. Open the vermouth, bow in the direction of the Front, and close it again. Two olives, not three, and a glass from the freezebox. These were the sacred objects of a Husband. Tie, Cadillac, martini. And then Dad would open the door and Faraday, the Irish setter, would yelp with waggy happiness and so would Martin. He'd be wearing a soft grey suit. He'd put his hat on the rack. Martin's mother, Rosemary, would stand on her tiptoes to kiss him in one of her good dresses, the lavender one with daises on the hem, or if it was a holiday, her sapphire-colored velvet. Her warm blonde hair would be perfectly set, and her lips would leave a gleaming red kiss-shape on his cheek. Dad wouldn't wipe it off. He'd greet his son with a firm handshake that told Martin all he needed to know: he was a man, his martini was good, his knots were strong.

Henry would slam the door to his bedroom upstairs and re-fuse to come down to supper. This pained Martin; the loud bang scuffed his heart. But he tried to understand his brother—after all, a Husband must possess great wells of understanding and compassion. Dad wasn't Henry's father. Pretending that he was probably scuffed something inside the elder boy too.

The profound and comforting sameness of those Husbanded weeks overwhelmed Martin's senses like the slightly greasy swirls of gin in that lovely triangular glass. The first night, they would have a roasting chicken with crackling golden skin. Rosemary had volunteered to raise several closely observed generations of an experimental breed called Sacramento Clouds: vicious, bright orange and oversized, dosed with palladium every fortnight, their eggs covered in rough calcium deposits like lichen. For this reason they could have a whole bird once a month. The rest of the week were New Vegetables from the Capsule Garden. Carrots, tomatoes, sprouts, potatoes, kale. Corn if it was fall and there hadn't been too many high-level days when no one could go out and tend the plants. But there was always that one delicious day when Father was at home and they had chicken.

After dinner, they would retire to the living room. Mom and Dad would have sherry and Martin would have a Springs Eternal Vita-Pop if he had been very good, which he always was. He liked the lime flavor best. They would watch *My Five Sons* for half an hour before Rosemary's Husband retired with her to bed. Martin didn't mind that. It was what Husbands were for. He liked to listen to the sounds of their lovemaking through the wall between their rooms. They were reassuring and good. They put him to sleep like a lullaby about better times.

And one week out of every four, Martin would ask his Father to take him to the city.

"I want to see where you work!"

"This is where I work, son," Father would always say in his rough-soft voice. "Right here."

Martin would frown and Dad would hold him tight. Husbands were not afraid of affection. They had bags of it to share. "I'll tell you what, Marty, if your Announcement goes by without a hitch, I'll take you to the city myself. March you right into the Office and show everyone what a fine boy Rosie and I made. Might even let you puff on a cigar."

And Martin would hug his Father fiercely, and Rosemary would smile over her fiber-optic knitting, and Henry would kick something upstairs. It was regular as a clock, and the clock was always right. Martin knew he'd be Announced, no problem. Piece of cake. Mom was super careful with the levels on their property. They planted Liberty Spinach. Martin was first under his desk every time the siren went off at school. After Henry's Announcement had gone so badly, he and Mom had installed a Friendlee Brand Geiger Unit every fifteen feet and the light-up aw-shucks faces had only turned into frowns and x-eyes a few times ever. There was no chance Martin could fail. Things were way better now. Not like when Henry was a kid. No, Martin would be Announced and he'd go to the city and smoke his cigar. He'd be ready. He'd be the best Husband anyone ever met.

Aaron Grudzinski liked to tell him it was all shit. That was, in fact, Aaron's favorite observation on nearly anything. Martin liked the way he swore, gutturally, like it really meant something. Grud was in Martin's year. He smoked Canadian cigarettes and nipped some kind of home-brewed liquor from his grey plastic Thermos. He'd egged Martin into a sip once. It tasted like dirt on fire.

"Look, didn't you ever wonder why they wait till you're fifteen to do it? Obviously they can test you anytime after you pop your first boner. As soon as you're brewing your own, yeah?" And Grud would shake his flask. "But no, they make this huge deal out of going down to Matthew House and squirting in a cup. The outfit, the banquet, the music, the filmstrips. It's all shit. Shit piled up into a pretty castle around a room where they give you a magazine full of the wholesome housewives of 1940 and tell you to do it for America. And you look down at the puddle at the bottom of the plastic tumbler they call your chalice, your chalice with milliliter measurements printed on the side, and you think: *That's all I am. Two to six milliliters of warm wet nothing.*" Grud spat a brown tobacco glob onto the dead grass of the baseball field. He knuckled at his eye, his voice getting raw. "Don't you get it? They have to give you hope. Well, I mean, they have to give *you* hope. I'm a lost cause. Three strikes before I got to bat. But you? They gotta build you up, like how everyone salutes Sgt. Dickhead on leave from the glowing shithole that is the great state of Arizona. If they didn't shake his hand and kiss his feet, he might start thinking it's not worth melting his face off down by the Glass. If you didn't think you could make it, you'd just kill yourself as soon as you could read the newspaper."

"I wouldn't," Martin whispered.

"Well, I would."

"But, Grud, there's so few of us left."

The school siren klaxoned. Martin bolted inside, sliding into the safe space under his desk like he was stealing home.

THE SHADOW EFFECT

Every Sunday Sylvie brought a couple of Vita-Pops out to the garage and set up her film projector in the hot dark. Her mother went to her Ladies' Auxiliary meeting from two to four o'clock. Sylvie swiped hors d'oeuvres and cookies from the official spread and waited in the shadows for Clark Baker to shake his mother and slip in the side door. The film projector had been a gift from her Father; the strips were Clark's, whose shutterbug brothers and uncles were all pulling time at the Front. Every Sunday they sat together and watched the light flicker and snap over a big white sheet nailed up over the shelves of soil-treatment equipment and Friendlee Brand gadgets stripped for parts. Every Sunday like church.

Clark was tall and shy, obsessed with cameras no less than any of his brothers. He wore striped shirts all the time, as if solid colors had never been invented. He kept reading Salinger even after the guy defected. Sometimes they held hands while they watched the movies. Mostly they didn't. It was bad enough that they were fraternizing at all. Clark already drinking Kool Koffee every morning. Sugar, no cream. Clark was a quiet, bookish black boy who would be sent to the Front within a year.

On the white sheet, they watched California melt.

It hadn't happened during the war. The Glass came after. This thing everyone did now was not called war. It was something else. Something that liquefied the earth out west and turned it into the Sea of Glass. On the sheet it looked like molten silver, rising and falling in something like waves. Turning the Grand Canyon into a soft grey whirlpool. Sylvie thought it was beautiful. Like something on the moon. In real life it had colors, and Sylvie dreamed of them. Red stone dissolving into an endless expanse of dark glass.

"There are more Japanese people in Utah than in Japan now," Clark whispered when the filmstrip rolled up into black and the filmmaker's logo. Sylvie flinched as if he'd cut her.

They didn't talk about her Presentation. It sat whitely, fatly in their future. Once Clark kissed her. Sylvie cried afterward.

"I'll write you," he said. "As long as I can write."

The growth index for their county was very healthy, and this was another reason Clark Baker should not have been holding her hand in the dark while men in ghostly astronaut suits probed the edges of the Glass on a clicking filmstrip. Every woman on the block had a new baby this year. They'd gotten a medal of achievement from President McCarthy in the spring. The Ladies' Auxiliary graciously accepted the key to the city. She suspected her Father had a great deal to do with this. When she was little, he had come home one week in four. Now it was three days in thirty. His department kept him working hard. He'd be there for her Presentation, though. No Father missed his daughter's debut.

Sylvie thought about Clark while her mother slipped satin-covered buttons through tiny loops. Their faces doubled in the mirror. His dark brown hand on hers. The Sea of Glass turning their faces silver.

"Mom," Sylvie said. Her voice was very soft in the morning, as if she was afraid to wake herself up. "What if I don't love my Husband? Isn't that . . . something important?"

Hannah sighed. Her mouth took a hard angle. "You're young, darling. You don't understand. What it was like before. We had to have them here all the time, every night. Never a moment when I wasn't working my knees through for my husband. The one before your Father. The children before you. Do you think we got to choose then? It wasn't about love. For some people, they could afford that. For me, well, my parents thought he was a very nice man. He had good prospects. I needed him. I could not work. I was a woman before the war, who would hire me? And to do what? Type or teach. Not to program punch-card machines. Not to crossbreed new strains of broccoli. Nothing that would occupy my mind. So I drowned my mind in children and in him and when the war came I was glad. He left and it was *me* going to work every morning, *me* deciding what happened to my money. So the war took them." She waved her hand in front of her eyes. "War always does that. I know you don't think so, but the program is the best part of a bad situation. A situation maybe so bad we cannot fix it. So you don't love him. Why would you look for love with a man? How could a man ever understand you? He who gets the cake cannot be friends with the girl who gets the crumbs." Sylvie's mother blushed. She whispered: "My Rita, you know, Rita who comes for tea and bridge and neptunium testing. She is good to me. Someone will be good to you. You will have your Auxiliary, your work, your children. One week in four a man will tell you what to do—but listen to me when I say they have much better manners than they used to. They say please now. They are interested in your life. They are so good with the babies." Hannah smoothed the lacy back of her daughter's Presentation gown. "Someday, my girl, either we will all die out and nothing will be left, or things will go back to the old ways and you will have men taking your body and soul apart to label the parts that belong to them. Enjoy this world. Either way, it will be brief."

Sylvie turned her painted, perfected face to her mother's. "Mom," she whispered. Sylvie had practiced. So much, so often.

She ordered the words in her head like dolls, hoped they were the right ones. Hoped they could stand up straight. "Watashi wa anata o shinjite ī nā." *I wish I could believe you.*

Hannah's dark eyes flew wide, and without a moment's hesitation, she slapped her daughter across the cheek. It wasn't hard, not meant to wound, certainly not to leave a mark on this day of all days, but it stung. Sylvie's eyes watered.

"Nidoto," her mother pleaded. "Never, *never* again."

GIMBELS: YOUR OFFICIAL FATHER'S DAY HEADQUARTERS!

PANORAMA SHOT *of the Gimbels flagship store with two cute kiddos front and center.* [Note to Casting: get us a boy and a girl, blonde, white, under ten, make sure the boy is taller than the girl. Put them in sailor suits, everyone likes that.] *The kids wave at the camera. Little Linda Sue speaks up.* [Note to Copy: Nope. The boy speaks first.] It's a beautiful June here in New York City, the greatest city on earth! *Jimmy throws his hands in the air and yells out:* And that means FATHER'S DAY! *Scene shift, kiddos are walking down a Gimbels aisle. We see toolboxes, ties, watches in a glass case, barbecue sets. Linda Sue picks up a watch and listens to it tick. Jimmy grabs a barbecue scraper and brandishes it. He says:* Come on down with your Mom and make an afternoon of it at the Brand New Gimbels Automat! Hot, pre-screened food in an instant! Gee wow! [Note to Copy: Hey, Stone, this is a government sponsored ad. If Gimbels wants to hawk their shitty Manhattan Meals they're going to have to actually pay for it. Have you ever tried one of those things? Tastes like a kick in the teeth.] *Linda Sue:* At Gimbels they have all the approved Father's Day products. *(Kids alternate lines)* Mr. Fix-It! Businessman! Coach! Backyard Cowboy! *Mr. Gimbel appears and selects a beautiful tie from the spring Priapus line. He hands it to Linda Sue and ruffles her hair. Mr Gimbel:* Now, kids, don't forget to register your gift with the Ladies' Auxiliary. We wouldn't want *your* Daddy to get two of the same gift!

How embarrassing! That's why Gimbels carries the complete Whole Father line, right next to the registration desk so your Father's Day is a perfect one. *Kids:* Thanks, Mr. Gimbel!

Mr. Gimbel spreads his arms wide and type stretches out between them in this year's Father's Day colors. [Note to Art Dept: It's seashell and buttercup this year, right? Please see Marketing concerning the Color Campaign. Pink and blue are pre-war. We're working with Gimbels to establish a White for Boys, Green for Girls tradition.]

Gimbels: Your One Stop Shop for a One of a Kind Dad.

Fade to white.

FLASH BLINDNESS

Martin wore the emerald green chevroned tie to his Announcement, even if it wasn't strictly within the dress code. Everything else was right down the line: light grey suit, shaved clean if shaving was on the menu, a dab of musky *Oil of Fecunditas* behind each ear from your friends at Spotless Corp. Black shoes, black socks, Spotless lavender talcum, teeth brushed three times with Pure Spearmint Toothpaste (*You're Sure with Spearmint!*). And his Father holding his hand, beaming with pride. Looking handsome and young as he always did.

Of course, there was another boy holding his other hand.

His name was Thomas. He had broad shoulders already, chocolate-colored hair and cool slate eyes that made him look terribly romantic. Martin tried not to let it bother him. He knew how the program worked. Where the other three weeks of the month took his Father. Obviously, there were other children, other wives, other homes. Other roasting chickens, other martinis. Other evening television shows on other channels. And that's all Thomas was: another channel. When you weren't watching a show, it just ceased to be. Clicked off. Fade to white. You couldn't be jealous of the people on those other channels. They had their own troubles and adventures, engrossing mysteries and stunning conclusions, cliffhangers and tune-in-next-weeks. It had nothing to do with Martin, or Rosemary, or Henry in his room. That was what it meant to be a Husband.

The three of them sat together in the backseat of the sleek grey Cadillac. An older lady drove them. She wore a smart cap and had wiry white hair, but her cheeks were still pink and round. Martin tried to look at her as a Husband would, even though a woman her age would never marry. After all, Husbands didn't get to choose. Martin's future wives—four to start with, that was standard, but if he did well, who knew?—wouldn't all be bombshells in pinup bathing suits. He had to practice looking at women, really seeing them, seeing what was good and true and gorgeous in them. The chauffeur had wonderful laugh lines around her eyes. Martin could tell they were laugh lines. And her eyes, when she looked in the rearview mirror, were a nice, cool green. She radioed to the dispatcher and her voice lilted along with a faint twinge of English accent. Martin could imagine her laughing with him, picking New Kale and telling jokes about the King. He imagined her naked, lying on a soft pink bed, soft like her pink cheeks. Her body would be the best kind of body: the kind that had borne children. Breasts that had nursed. Legs that had run after misbehaving little ones. He could love that body. The sudden hardness between his legs held no threat, only infinite love and acceptance, a Husband's love.

When I think about how good I could be, my heart stops, Martin thought as the space between his neighborhood and the city smeared by. The sun seared white through dead black trees. But somewhere deep in them there was a green wick. Martin knew it. He had a green wick too. *I will remember every date. Every wife will be so special and I will love her and our children. I will make her martinis. I will roast the chicken so she doesn't have to. When I am with one of them I will turn off all other channels in my mind. I can keep it straight and separate. I will study so hard, so that I know how to please. It will be my only vocation, to be devoted. And if they the women of Elm St. or Oak Lane or Birch Drive find love with each other when I am gone, I will be happy for them because there is never enough love. I will draw them happy and they will be happy. The world will be green again. Everything will be okay.*

It all seemed to happen very fast. Thomas and Martin and a dozen other boys listened to a quintet play Mendelssohn. The mayor gave a speech. They watched a recorded message from President McCarthy that had to be pretty old because he still sported a good head of hair. Finally, a minister stood up with a lovely New Tabernacle Bible in her one good hand. The other was shriveled, boneless, a black claw in her green vestments. The pages of the Bible shone with gilt. A ribbonmark hung down, and it was very red in the afternoon flares. She did not lay it on a lectern. She carried the weight in her hands and read from the Gospel of Pseudo-Matthew, which Martin already knew by heart. The minister's maple-syrup contralto filled the vaults of Matthew House.

"And when Mary had come to her fourteenth year, the high priest announced to all that the virgins who were reared in the Temple and who had reached the age of their womanhood should return to their own and be given in lawful marriage. When the High Priest went in to take counsel with God, a voice came forth from the oratory for all to hear, and it said that of all of the marriageable men of the House of David who had not yet taken a wife, each should bring a rod and lay it upon the altar, that one of the rods would burst into flower and upon it the Holy Ghost would come to rest in the form of a Dove, and that he to whom this rod belonged would be the one to whom the virgin Mary should be espoused. Joseph was among the men who came, and he placed his rod upon the altar, and straightaway it burst into bloom and a Dove came from Heaven and perched upon it, whereby it was manifest to all that Mary should become the wife of Joseph."

Martin's eyes filled with tears. He felt a terrible light in his chest. For a moment he was sure everyone else would see it streaming out of him. But no, the minister gave him a white silk purse and directed him to a booth with a white velvet curtain. Inside, silence.

Dim, dusty light. Martin opened the purse and pulled out the chalice—a plastic cup with measurements printed on it, just like Grud said. With it lay a few old photographs—women from before the war, with so much health in their faces Martin could hardly bear to look at them. Their skin was so clear. *She's dead,* he thought. *Statistically speaking, that woman with the black hair and heart-shaped face and polka-dotted bikini is dead. Vaporized in Seattle or Phoenix or Los Angeles. That was where they used to make pictures, in Los Angeles. This girl is dead.*

Martin couldn't do it. This was about life. Everything, no matter how hard and strange, was toward life. He could not use a dead girl that way. Instead, he shut his eyes. He made his pictures, quick pencil lines glowing inside him. The chauffeur with her pink cheeks and white hair. The minister with kind voice and brown eyes and her shriveled hand, which was awful, but wasn't she alive and good? Tammy, the girl from the Victory Brand Capsule Garden commercials in her star-spangled dress. A girl with red hair who lived two blocks over and was so pretty that looking at her was like getting punched in the chest. He drew in bold, bright lines the home he was going to make, bigger than himself, bigger than the war, as big as the world.

Martin's body convulsed with the tiny, private detonation of his soul. His vision blurred into a hot colorless flash.

BLAST WIND

Sylvie's mother helped her into long white gloves. They sat together in a long pearl-colored Packard and did not speak. Sylvie had nothing to say. Let her mother be uncomfortable. A visceral purple sunset colored the western sky, even at two in the afternoon. Sylvie played the test in her head like a filmstrip. When it actually started happening to her, it felt no more real than a picture on a sheet.

The mayor gave a speech. They watched a recorded message

from President McCarthy's pre-war daughter Tierney, a pioneer in the program, one of the first to volunteer. *Our numbers have been depleted by the Germans, the Japanese, and now the Godless Russians. Of the American men still living only 12 percent are fertile. But we are not Communists. We cannot become profligate, wasteful, decadent. We must maintain our moral way of life. As little as possible should change from the world your mothers knew—at least on the surface. And with time, what appears on the surface will penetrate to the core, and all will be restored. We will not sacrifice our way of life.*

A minister with a withered arm read that Pseudo-Matthew passage Tierney had dredged up out of apocrypha to the apocrypha, about the rods and the flowers, and Sylvie had never felt it was one of the Gospel's more subtle moments. The minister blessed them. They are flowers. They are waiting for the Dove.

The doctors were women. One was Mrs. Drexler, who lived on their cul-de-sac and always made rum balls for the neighborhood Christmas cookie exchange. She was kind. She warmed up her fingers before she examined Sylvie. *White gloves for her, white gloves for me*, Sylvie thought, and suppressed a giggle. She turned her head to one side and focused on a stained-glass lamp with kingfishers on it, piercing their frosted breasts with their beaks. She went somewhere else in her mind until it was over. Not a happy place, just a place. Somewhere precise and clean without any Spotless Corp. products where Sylvie could test soil samples methodically. Rows of black vials, each labeled, dated, sealed.

They took her blood. A butterfly of panic fluttered in her—will they know? Would the test show her mother, practicing her English until her accent came out clean as acid paper? Running from a red Utah sky even though there was no one left to shoot at her? Only half, white enough to pass, curling her hair like it would save her? Sylvie shut her eyes. She said her mother's name three times in her mind. The secret, talismanic thing that only they together knew. *Hidaka Hanako. Hidaka Hanako. Hidaka Hanako. Don't be silly. Japan isn't a virus they can see wiggling in your cells. Mom's documents are flawless. No alarm will go off in the centrifuge.*

And none did.

She whizzed through the intelligence exams—what a joke. *Calculate the drag energy of the blast wind given the following variables.* Please. Other girls milled around her in their identical lace dresses. The flowers in their hair were different. Their sashes all red. Red on white, like first-aid kits floating through her peripheral vision. They went from medical to placement testing to screening. They nodded shyly to each other. In five years, Sylvie would know all their names. They would be her Auxiliary. They would play bridge. They would plan block parties. They would have telephone trees. Some of them would share a Husband with her, but she would never know which. That was what let the whole civilized fiction roll along. You never knew, you never asked. Men had a different surname every week. Only the Mrs. Drexlers of the neighborhood knew it all, the knots and snags of the vital genetics. Would she share with the frosted blonde who loved botany or the redheaded math genius who made her own cheese? Or maybe none of them. It all depended on the test. Some of these girls would score low in their academics or have some unexpressed, unpredictable trait revealed in the great forking family trees pruned by Mrs. Drexler and the rest of them. They would get Husbands in overalls, with limited allowances. They would live in houses with old paint and lead shielding instead of Gamma Glass. Some of them would knock their Presentation out of the park. They'd get Husbands in grey suits and silk ties, who went to offices in the city during the day, who gave them compression chamber diamonds for their birthdays. As little as possible should change.

Results were quick these days. Every year faster. But not so quick that they did not have luncheon provided while the experts performed their tabulations. Chicken salad sandwiches—how the skinny ones gasped at the taste of mayonnaise! Assam tea, watercress, lemon curd and biscuits. An impossible fairy feast.

"I hope I get a Businessman," said the girl sitting next to Sylvie. Her bouffant glittered with illegal setting spray. "I couldn't bear it if I had to live on Daisy Drive."

"Who cares?" said Sylvie, and shoved a whole chicken salad triangle into her mouth. She shouldn't have said anything. Her silence bent for one second and out comes nonsense that would get her noticed. Would get her remembered.

"Well, *I* care, you *cow*," snapped Bouffant. Her friends smiled behind their hands, concealing their teeth. *In primates, baring the teeth is a sign of aggression,* Sylvie thought idly. She flashed them a broad, cold smile. *All thirty-two, girls, drink it in.*

"I think it's clear what room *you'll* be spending the evening in," Bouffant sneered, oblivious to Sylvie's primate signals.

But Sylvie couldn't stop. "At best, you'll spend 25 percent of your time with him. You'll get your rations the same as everyone. You'll get your vouchers for participating in the program and access to top make-work contracts. What difference does it make who you snag? You know this is just pretend, right? A very big, very lush, very elaborate dog breeding program."

Bouffant narrowed her eyes. Her lips went utterly pale. "I hope you turn out to be barren as a rock. Just *rotted away inside*," she hissed. The group of them stood up in a huff and took their tea to another table. Sylvie shrugged and ate her biscuit. "Well, that's no way to think if you want to restore America," she said to no one at all. What was the matter with her? *Shut up, Sylvie.*

Mrs. Drexler put a warm hand on her shoulder, materializing out of nowhere. The doctor who loved rum balls laid a round green chip on the white tablecloth. Bouffant saw it across the room and glared hard enough to put a hole through her skull at forty yards.

Sylvie was fertile. At least, there was nothing obviously wrong with her. She turned the chip over. The other side was red. Highest marks. *Blood and leaves. Red on white. The world is red and I am red forever.* One of Bouffant's friends was holding a black chip and crying, deep and horrible. Sylvie floated. Unreal. It wasn't real. It was ridiculous. It was a filmstrip. A recording made years ago when Brussels sprouts were small and the sunset could be rosy and gentle.

FADE IN on Mrs. Drexler in a dance hall with a white on white checkerboard floor. She's wearing a sequin torch-singer dress. Bright pink. She pumps a giant star-spangled speculum like a parade-master's baton. Well, hello there, Sylvia! It's your big day! Should I say Hidaka Sakiko? I only want you to be comfortable, dear. Let's see what you've won!

Sylvie and the other green-chip girls were directed into another room whose walls were swathed in green velvet curtains. A number of men stood lined up against the wall, chatting nervously among themselves. Each had a cedar rod in one hand. They held the rods awkwardly, like old men's canes. A piano player laid down a slow foxtrot for them. Champagne was served. A tall boy with slightly burned skin, a shiny pattern of pink across his cheek, takes her hand, first in line. In Sylvie's head, the filmstrip zings along.

WIDE SHOT of Mrs. Drexler yanking on a rope-pull curtain. She announces: Behind Door Number One we have Charles Patterson, six foot one, Welsh/Danish stock, blond/blue, scoring high in both logic and empathy, average sperm count 19 million per milliliter! This hot little number has a reserved parking spot at the Office! Of course, when I say "Office," I mean the upper gentlemen's club, brandy and ferns on the thirty-fifth floor, cigars and fraternity and polished teak walls. A little clan to help each other through the challenges of life in the program—only another Husband can really understand. Our productive heartthrobs are too valuable to work! Stress has been shown to lower semen quality, Sylvie! But as little as possible should change. If you take the Office from a man, you'll take his spirit. And what's behind Door Number Two?

Sylvie shut her eyes. The real Mrs. Drexler was biting into a sugar cookie and sipping her champagne. She opened them again—and a stocky kind-eyed boy had already cut in for the next song. He wore an apple blossom in his lapel. For everlasting love, Broome

County's official flower for the year. The dancing Mrs. Drexler in her mind hooted with delight, twirling her speculum.

TIGHT SHOT of Door Number Two. Mrs Drexler snaps her fingers and cries: Why, it's Douglas Owens! Five foot ten, Irish/Italian, that's *very* exciting! Brown/brown, scoring aces in creative play and nurturing, average sperm count 25 million per milliliter—oh ho! Big, strapping boy! *Mrs. Drexler slaps him lightly on the behind. Her eyes gleam.* He's a Businessman as well, nothing but the best for our Sylvie, our prime stock Sylvie/Sakiko! He'll take his briefcase every day and go sit in his club with the other Husbands, and maybe he loves you and maybe he finds real love with them the way you'll find it with your friend Bouffant in about two years. Who can tell? It's so *thrilling* to speculate! It's not like men and women got along so well before, anyway. Take my wife, please! Why I oughta! To hell with the whole mess. Give it one week a month. You do unpleasant things one week out of four and don't think twice. Who cares?

Someone handed her a glass of champagne. Sylvie wrapped her real, solid fingers around it. She felt dizzy. A new boy had taken up her hand and put his palm around her waist. The dance quickened. Still a foxtrot, but one with life in it. She looked at the wheel and spin of faces—white faces, wide, floor-model faces. Sylvie looked for Clark. Anywhere, everywhere, his kind face moving among the perfect bodies, his kind face with a silver molten earth undulating across his cheeks, flickering, shuddering. But he wasn't there. He would never be there. It would never be Clark with a cedar rod and a sugar cookie. Black boys didn't get Announced. Not Asians, not refugees, not Sylvie if anyone guessed. They got shipped out. They got a ticket to California. To Utah.

As little as possible should change.

No matter how bad it got, McCarthy and his Brothers just couldn't let a nice white girl (like Sylvie, like Sylvie, like the good floor-model part of Sylvie that fenced in the red, searing thing at the heart of her) get ruined that way. (If they knew, if they knew. Did the conservative-suit warm-glove Mrs. Drexler guess? Did it show in her dancing?) Draw the world the way you want it. Draw it and it will be.

Sylvie tried to focus on the boy she was dancing with. She was supposed to be making a decision, settling, rooting herself forever into this room, the green curtains, the sugar cookies, the foxtrot.

QUICK CUT to Mrs. Drexler. She spins around and claps her hands. She whaps her speculum on the floor three times and a thin kid with chocolate-colored hair and slate eyes sweeps aside his curtain. She crows: But wait, we haven't opened Doooooor Number Three! Hello, Thomas Walker! Six foot even, Swiss/Polish—ooh, practically Russian! How exotic! I smell a match! Brown/grey, top marks across the board, average sperm count a spectacular 29 million per milliliter! You're just showing off, young man! Allow me to shake your hand!

Sylvie jittered back and forth as the filmstrip caught. The champagne settled her stomach. A little. Thomas spun her around shyly as the music flourished. He had a romantic look to him. Lovely chocolate brown hair. He was saying something about being interested in the animal repopulation projects going on in the Plains States. His voice was sweet and a little rough and fine, fine, this one is fine, it doesn't matter, who cares, he'll never sit in a garage with me and watch the bombs fall on the sheet with the hole in the corner. Close your eyes, spin around three times, point at one of them and get it over with.

IRIS TRANSITION to Mrs. Drexler doing a backflip in her sequined dress. She lands in splits. Mr. and Mrs. Wells and Walker invite you to the occasion of their children's wedding!

Sylvie pulled the red, thornless rose and snowdrops from her hair and tied their ribbon around Thomas's rod. She remembered to smile. Thomas himself kissed her, first on the forehead and then on the mouth. A lot of couples seemed to be kissing now. The music had stopped. It's over, it's over, Sylvie thought. Maybe I can still see Clark today. It takes time to plan a wedding.

Voices buzzed and spiked behind her. Mrs. Drexler was hurrying over; her face was dark.

ZOOM on Mrs. Drexler: Wait, sorry, wait! I'm sorry, we seem to have hit a snag! It appears Thomas and Sylvie here are a little too close for comfort. They should never have been paired at the same Announcement. Our fault, entirely! Sylvie's Father has been such a boon to the neighborhood! Doing his part! Unfortunately, the great nation of the United States does not condone incest, so you'll have to trade Door Number Three for something a little more your speed. This sort of thing does happen! That's why we keep such excellent records! CROSS-REFERENCING! Thank you! *Mrs. Drexler bows. Roses land at her feet.*

Sylvie shut her eyes. The strip juddered; she was crying tracks through her Spotless Corp. Pressed Powder and it was not a film, it was happening. Mrs. Drexler was wearing a conservative brown suit with a gold dove-shaped pin on the lapel and waving a long-stemmed peony for masculine bravery. Thomas was her brother, somehow; there had been a mix-up and he was her brother and other arrangements would have to be made. The boys and girls in a ballroom with her stared and pointed, paired off safely. Sylvie looked up at Thomas. He stared back, young and sad and confused. The snowdrops and roses had fallen off his rod onto the floor. Red on white. Bouffant was practically climbing over Douglas Owens 25 million per milliliter like a tree.

In four years Sylvie would be Mrs. Charles Patterson 19 million per. It was over and they began to dance. Charles was a swell dancer. He promised to be sweet to her when he got through with training and they were married. He promised to make everything as normal as possible. As little as possible should change. The quintet struck up Mendelssohn.

Sylvie pulled her silence over her and it was good.

Fade to white.

CLOSE-UP of a nice-looking Bobby, a real lantern-jaw, straight-dealing, chiseled type. [Note to Casting: maybe we should consider VP Kroc for this spot. Hair pomade knows no demographic. Those idiots at Brylcreem want to corner the Paternal market? Fine. Let them have their little slice of the pie. Be a nice bit of PR for the reelection campaign too. Humanize the son of a bitch. Ray Kroc, All-American, Brother to the Common Man. Even he suffers symptomatic hair loss. Whatever—you get the idea. Talk to Copy.] *Bobby's getting dressed in the morning, towel around his healthy, muscular body.* [Note to Casting: if we go with Kroc here we'll have to find a body double.] *Looks at himself in the mirror and strokes a five-o'clock shadow.*

FEMALE VOICE OVER: Do you wake up in the morning to a sink full of disappointment?

PAN DOWN to a clean white sink. Clumps of hair litter the porcelain. [Note to Art Dept: Come on, Stone, don't go overboard. No more than twenty strands.] *Bobby rubs the top of his head. His expression is crestfallen.*

VOICE OVER: Well, no more! Now with the radiation-blocking power of lead, All-New Formula Samson Brand Hair Pomade can make you an All-New Man.

Bobby squirts a generous amount of Samson Brand from his tube and rubs it on his head. A blissful smile transforms his face.

VOICE OVER: That feeling of euphoria and well-being lets you know it works! Samson Pomades and Creams have been infused with our patented mood-boosters, vitamins, and just a dash of caffeine to help you start your day out right!

PAN DOWN to the sink. Bobby turns the faucet on; the clumps of hair wash away. When we pan back up, Bobby has a full head of glossy, thick, styled hair. [Note to Art Dept: Go whole hog. When the camera comes back put the VP in a full suit, with the perfect hair—a wig, obviously—and the Senate gavel in his hand. I like to see a little more imagination from you, Stone. Not a good quarter for you.]

VOICE OVER: Like magic, Samson Brand Pomade gives you the confidence you need. [Note to Copy: not sure about 'confidence' here. What about 'peace of mind'? We're already getting shit from the FDA about dosing Brothers with caffeine and uppers. Probably don't want to make it sound like the new formula undoes Arcadia.]

He gives the camera a thumbs-up. [Note to Art Dept: Have him offer the camera a handshake. Like our boy Ray is offering America a square deal.]

Bold helvetica across mid-screen:

Samson Guards Your Strength.

Fade to white.

TEN GREYS

Martin watched his brother. The handsome Thomas. The promising Thomas. The fruitful and multiplying Thomas. Twenty-nine million per mil Thomas. Their father (24 million) didn't even try to fight his joyful tears as he pinned the golden dove on his son's chest. His good son. His true son. For Thomas the Office in the city. For Thomas the planning and pleasing and roasted chickens and martinis. For Thomas the children as easy as pencil drawings.

For Martin Stone, 2 million per milliliter and most of those dead, a package. In a nice box, to be certain. Irradiated teak. It didn't matter now anyway. Martin knew without looking what lay nestled in the box. A piece of paper and a bottle. The paper was an ordnance unknown until he opened the box. It was a lottery. The only way to be fair. It was his ticket.

It might request that he present himself at his local Induction Center at 0900 at the close of the school year. To be shipped out to the Front, which by then might be in Missouri for all anyone knew. He'd suit up and boot it across the twisted, bubbled moonscape of the Sea of Glass. An astronaut. Bouncing on the pulses from Los

Alamos to the Pacific. He would never draw again. By Christmas, he wouldn't have the fine motor skills.

Or it would request just as politely that he arrange for travel to Washington for a battery of civic exams and placement in government service. Fertile men couldn't think clearly, didn't you know? All that sperm. Can't be rational with all that business sloshing around in there. Husbands couldn't run things. They were needed for more important work. The most important work. Only Brothers could really view things objectively. Big picture men. And women, Sisters, those gorgeous black chip girls with 3-Alpha running cool and sweet in their veins. Martin would probably pull Department of Advertising and Information. Most people did. Other than Defense, it was the biggest sector going. The bottle would be Arcadia. For immediate dosage, and every day for the rest of his life. All sex shall be potentially reproductive. Every girl screwing a Brother is failing to screw a Husband and that just won't do. They said it tasted like burnt batteries if you didn't put it in something. The first bottle would be the pure stuff, though. Provided by Halcyon, Your Friend in the Drug Manufacturing Business. Martin would remember it, the copper sear on the roof of his mouth. After that, a whole aisle of choices. Choices, after all, make you who you are. Arcadia or Kool. Brylcreem or Samson.

Don't worry, Martin. It's a relief, really. Now you can really get to work. Accomplish something. Carve out your place. Sell the world to the world. You could work your way into the Art Department. Keep drawing babies in carriages. Someone else's perfect quads, their four faces laughing at you forever from glossy pages.

Suddenly Martin found himself clasped tight in his Father's arms. Pulling the box out of his boy's hands, reading the news for him, putting it aside. His voice came as rough as warm gin and Martin could hardly breathe for the strength of his Father's embrace.

Thomas Walker squeezed his brother's hand. Martin did not squeeze back.

VELOCITY MULTIPLIED BY DURATION

Sylvie's Father was with them that week. He was proud. They bought a chicken from Mrs. Stone and killed it together, as a family. The head popped off like a cork. Sylvie stole glances at him at the table. She could see it now. The chocolate hair. The tallness. Hannah framed her Presentation Scroll and hung it over the fireplace.

Sylvie flushed her Spotless trousseaux down the toilet.

She wasn't angry. You can't get angry just because the world's so much bigger than you and you're stuck in it. That's just the face of it, cookie. A poisoned earth, a sequined dress, a speculum you can play like the spoons. Sylvie wasn't angry. She was silent. Her life was Mrs. Patterson's life. People lived in all kinds of messes. She could make rum balls. And treat soil samples and graft cherry varieties and teach some future son or daughter Japanese three weeks a month where no one else could hear. She could look up Bouffant's friend and buy her a stiff drink. She could enjoy the brief world of solitude and science and birth like red skies dawning. Maybe. She had time.

It was all shit, like that Polish kid who used to hang around the soda fountain kept saying. It was definitely all shit.

On Sunday she went out to the garage again. Vita-Pops and shadows. Clark slipped in like light through a crack. He had a canister of old war footage under his arm. Stalingrad, Berlin, Ottawa. Yellow shirt with green stripes. Nagasaki and Tokyo, vaporizing like hearts in a vast, wet chest. The first retaliation. Seattle, San Francisco, Los Angeles. Clark reached out and held her hand. She didn't squeeze back. The silent detonations on the white sheet like sudden balloons, filling up and up and up. It looked like the inside of Sylvie.

"This is my last visit," Clark said. "School year's over." His voice sounded far away, muffled, like he didn't even know he was talking. "Car's coming in the morning. Me and Grud are sharing a ride to Induction. I think we get a free lunch."

Sylvie wanted to scream at him. She sucked down her pop, drowned the scream in bubbles.

"I love you," whispered Clark Baker.

On the sheet, the Golden Gate Bridge vanished.

Sylvie rolled the reel back. They watched it over and over. A fleck of nothing dropping out of the sky and then, then the flash, a devouring, brain-boiling, half-sublime sheet of white that blossomed like a flower out of a dead rod, an infinite white everything that obliterated the screen.

Fade to black.

And over the black, a cheerful fat man giving the thumbs up to Sylvie, grinning:

Buy Freedom Brand Film! It's A-OK!

THE EMPEROR OF TSUKAYAMA PARK

When first the word was spoken, I heard:
Tsuki-yama—Lord Moon.
    And for me, the moon settled onto a dais, with
sixteen-pointed chrysanthemums in his phosphor-hands,
topknot oiled with seaweed and orange,
his *hakama* fringed in silver worms
which wove on and on,
flooding the nightingale-floor with silk.

The folds of his sleeves creased blue and black
in signet-shadows, descending like stairs to me,
in a poor, threadbare *yukata*,
my sallow Western skin protruding,
forehead pressed to his white *tatami*.
    For me, the moon extended a branch of heavy plums
and with well-water eyes forgave my ignorance of protocol,
my botched *obi*, my hair unpinned and ragged.

When winter came to Tsukayama Park,
    it seemed to me that the strange-limbed tigers

of his wall-hangings
rumbled like clouds, and I was permitted to watch
the sparrows spiral up to his ashen ear. Under his cratered
    arms,
I knelt, and whispered tears into the *hiragana* of my
    palm-lines,
obscuring the text with salt and snow.

    For him, I was always penitent.
I did not question his rule over the cherry trees, the green
    tide,
the steam of tea in a glazed cup. I allowed him to stifle
my breath in twelve layers of white silk, to paint me a new
    mouth,
to fold back my hair in beryl combs
that cut my scalp with piscine teeth. For him, I pressed out my
    pride,
flat as a river, and bowed my face to the floor.

When summer came to Tsukayama Park
    it seemed to me that his voice was the thrust-cry of
        cicadas,
that the wind beat drums of star-hide, that I had
learnt the angle of the closed mouth
well enough to pass for one of his own.

But in the midst of my prostrations, my rain-hymns,
the steeping of my braids in inkwells,
I heard a woman laugh at me.
She said that the word was
Tsukayama—top of the hill—nothing more.
    And for me, the moon was excised from the sky.

I had no grace left but my face flattened into sun-cracked
    dirt,

no patron but the feet of a false moon,
evaporated into plain grass and a stone stair.

My kimono dissolved to water,
and the sparrows turned in shame
from my nakedness.

KILLSWITCH

In the spring of 1989 the Karvina Corporation released a curious game, whose dissemination among American students that fall was swift and furious, though its popularity was ultimately short-lived.

The game was *Killswitch*.

On the surface it was a variant on the mystery or horror survival game, a precursor to the *Myst* and *Silent Hill* franchises. The narrative showed the complexity for which Karvina was known, though the graphics were monochrome, vague grey and white shapes against a black background. Slow MIDI versions of Czech folk songs played throughout. Players could choose between two avatars: an invisible demon named Ghast or a visible human woman, Porto. Play as Ghast was considerably more difficult due to his total invisibility, and players were highly liable to restart the game as Porto after the first level, in which it was impossible to gauge jumps or aim. However, Ghast was clearly the more powerful character—he had fire-breath and a coal-steam attack, but as it was above the skill level of most players to keep track of where a fire-breathing, poison-dispensing invisible imp was on their screens once the fire and steam had run out, Porto became more or less the default.

Porto's singular ability was seemingly random growth—she expanded and contracted in size throughout the game. A Kansas engineering grad claimed to have figured out the pattern involved, but for reasons which will become obvious, his work was lost.

Porto awakens in the dark with wounds in her elbows, confused. Seeking a way out, she ascends through the levels of a coal mine in which it is slowly revealed she was once an employee, investigating its collapse and beset on all sides by demons similar to Ghast, as well as dead foremen, coal-golems, and demonic inspectors from the Sovatik corporation, whose boxy bodies are clothed in red, the only color in the game. The environment, though primitive, becomes genuinely uncanny as play progresses. There are no "bosses" in any real sense—Porto must simply move physically through tunnels to reach subsequent levels while her size varies wildly through inter-level spaces.

The story that emerges through Porto's discovery of magnetic tapes, files, mutilated factory workers who were once her friends, and deciphering an impressively complex code inscribed on a series of iron axes players must collect (This portion of the game was almost laughably complex and defeated many players until "Porto881" posted the cipher to a Columbia BBS. Attempts to contact this player have been unsuccessful, and the username is no longer in use on any known service.) is that the foremen, under pressure to increase coal production, began to falsify reports of malfunctions and worker malfeasance in order to excuse low output, which incited a Sovatik inspection. Officials were dispatched, one for each miner, and an extraordinary story of torture unfolds, with fuzzy and indistinct graphics of red-coated men standing over workers, inserting small knives into their joints whenever production slowed. (Admittedly, this is not a very subtle critique of Soviet-era industrial tactics, and as the town of Karvina itself was devastated by the departure of the coal industry, more than one thesis has interpreted Killswitch as a political screed.)

After solving the axe code, Porto finds and assembles a tape recorder, on which a male voice tells her that the fires of the earth had risen up in their defense and flowed into the hearts of the decrepit, pre-revolution equipment they used and wakened them to avenge the workers. It is generally assumed that the "fires of the earth" are demons like Ghast, coal fumes and gassy bodies inhabiting the old machines. The machines themselves are so "big" that the graphics elect to show only two or three gear teeth or a conveyor belt rather than the entire apparatus. The machines drove the inspectors mad, and they disappeared into caverns with their knives (only to emerge to plague Porto, of course). The workers were often crushed and mangled in the onslaught of machines, who were neither graceful nor discriminating. Porto herself was knocked into a deep chasm by a grief-stricken engine, and her fluctuating size, if it is real and not imagined, is implied to be the result of poisonous fumes inhaled there.

What follows is the most cryptic and intuitive part of the game. There is no logical reason to proceed in the "correct" way, and again it was Porto881 who came to the rescue of the fledgling *Killswitch* community. In the chamber behind the tape recorder is a great furnace where coal was once rendered into coke. There are no clues as to what she is intended to do in this room. Players attempted nearly everything, from immolating her to continuing to process coal as if the machines had never risen up. Porto881 hit upon the solution and posted it to the Columbia boards. If Porto ingests the raw coke, she will find her body under control, and can go on to fight her way out of the final levels of the mine, which are impassable in her giant state, clutching the tape containing this extraordinary story. However, as she crawls through the final tunnel to emerge aboveground, the screen goes suddenly white.

Killswitch, by design, deletes itself upon player completion of the game. It is not recoverable by any means; all trace of it is removed from the user's computer. The game cannot be copied. For all intents and purposes it exists only for those playing it and then ceases to be entirely. One cannot replay it, unlocking further secrets or narrative pathways; one cannot allow another to play it; and perhaps most importantly, it is impossible to experience the game all the way to the end as both Porto and Ghast.

Predictably, player outcry was enormous. Several routes to solve the problem were pursued, with no real efficacy. The first and most common was to simply buy more copies of the game, but Karvina Corp. released only five thousand copies and refused to press further editions. The following is an excerpt from their May 1990 press release:

> *Killswitch* was designed to be a unique playing experience: like reality, it is unrepeatable, unretrievable, and illogical. One might even say ineffable. Death is final; death is complete. The fates of Porto and her beloved Ghast are as unknowable as our own. It is the desire of the Karvina Corporation that this be so, and we ask our customers to respect that desire. Rest assured Karvina will continue to provide games of the highest quality to the West, and that *Killswitch* is merely one among our many wonders.

This did not have the intended effect. The word "beloved" piqued the interest of committed, even obsessive players, as Ghast is not present in any portion of Porto's narrative. A rush to find the remaining copies of the game ensued, with the intent of playing as Ghast and discovering the meaning of Karvina's cryptic word. The most popular theory was that Ghast would at some point become the fumes inhaled by Porto, changing her size and beginning her adventure. Some thought this was wishful thinking, that if only Ghast's early levels were passable one would somehow be able to play as both simultaneously. However, by this time no further copies appeared to be available in retail outlets. Players who had not yet completed the game attempted Ghast's levels frequently, but the difficulty of actually playing this enigmatic avatar persisted, and no player has ever claimed to have finished the game as Ghast. One by one, the lure of Porto's lost, unearthly world drew them back to her, and one by one, they were compelled toward the finality of the vast white screen.

To find any copy usable today is an almost unfathomably rare occurrence; a still shrink-wrapped copy was sold at auction in 2005 for $733,000 to Yamamoto Ryuichi of Tokyo. It is entirely possible that Yamamoto's is the last remaining copy of the game. Knowing this, Yakamoto had intended to open his play to all enthusiasts, filming and uploading his progress. However, to date, the only film that has surfaced is a one minute and forty-five second clip of a haggard Yamamoto at his computer, the avatar-choice screen visible over his right shoulder.

Yamamoto is crying.

MEMOIRS OF A GIRL WHO FAILED
TO BE BORN FROM A PEACH

In the year that they rented the Los Angeles apartment
with turn of the century plumbing,
when her hair was cropped short, the bleach rinsed out,
when he still read Fitzgerald,
they had given up hope of a child.
   I appeared without warning,
like the samurai Momotaro, who floated up
into his mother's Tuesday washing
packed into the pulpy womb of a yellow peach.

And like him, I also cried out to my father:
Wait, wait!
when he thoughtlessly drew a knife from the kitchen drawer
to slice the fruit in quarters.

   It would be nice to think that he paused,
listening to my sugar-buried exhortation,
that I sprang from the bed of wet gold
in a helmet of antlers and a bamboo *kusazuri*.

If I had leapt from the honey-bed and kissed my mother's ear,
then I, too, might have given bean-dumplings
to the monkey,
the pheasant,
the spotted dog.

　　We might have gone together, then,
trampling the grass with filial feet.
We might have built a raft of palm fronds, held fast
by a paste of betel and coconut,
and sailing across the water,
we would have slaughtered in seven clean strokes
the giants of Ogre Island,
whose flesh was red,
and blue,
and black.

I would have brought home to them the magic hammer,
which produced gold whenever it struck the earth.

Perhaps the peach-musculature muffled my voice,
or perhaps their neighbor, who had lived alone
in her little room for 50 years,
was playing the piano again,
her foot death-heavy on the reverberating pedal—
　　but my father cut the peach with two clean strokes,
each slice falling onto the cutting board at the same moment
　　like four wasting moons.

THE GIRL WITH TWO SKINS

I.

On your knees between moon-green shoots,
beside a sack of seed, a silver can, a white spade,
a ball is tucked into the bustle of your skirt:
like a pearl
but not a pearl.
You pulled it up
round as a beet from between the mint and the beans
where I had sunk it in the earth,
as though I fished
for loam-finned, moss-gilled coelacanth
at the bottom of the world.
I thought it safe.

I crawl to you on belly henna-bright,
teeth out,
scratching the basil sprouts—
eyes flash phosphor. In the late light,
slant gold light,
you must see

the old tail echo
beneath my muddy dress:
two, three, nine.

I howl against the barking churchbells:
Give it back, give it back,
I need it.

II.

Once I skulked snoutwise through scrap-iron forests,
And to each man with his silver pail scowled:

You are not beautiful enough
to make me human.

I had a fox's education:
rich coffee grounds in every house gutter,
mice whose bones were sweet to suck,
stolen bread and rainwater on whiskers:
slow theogonies of bottle caps and house cats.

I crouched, the color of rusted stairs,
and to each boy who chased me
through rotted wheat laughed:

You are not beautiful enough
to turn my tail to feet!

But this is a story,
and in a story
there is always someone
beautiful enough.

In a wood I found you
in the classical way,

a girl in a dress with a high hem,
ribbons in her teeth,
honey on her thumbs.

(Damn all of you. All your red hair
just enough like fur,
Damn all your small mouth,
your damp smell,
Damn all your pianos and stitching hoops.
Had I but paws enough to stamp out
your every spoken word like snow!)

You spooled out lessons
like an older sister:
Make your waist like this,
indicating curve.
Make your eyes like this,
indicating blue.
Make your face
make your skin
make your clever, clever hands,
make them this way,
indicating civilized,
indicating soft, your own,
your freckled breast linen-bound.

The old vixens, with their scabby,
mushroom-strung claws,
only said to run from boys,
and you looked so thick and pure,
like the inside
of a bone.

III.

I lashed my tail to my waist
in your gold-wood kitchen,

ridiculous in blue silk,
with cornflowers in my ears.
We bent over squash soup and sour cherries,
you put your hands over mine
to show me how to crease dough
over a silver pan.
I bit your cheek at teatime;
you smelled all day of my musk.

No, you laughed like sugar stirring,
your feet are too black,
your teeth are so sharp!
Can you not stand up straight
in my old dresses?
Can you not make your flesh
like mine?

Shamed, fur flamed across my cheek,
but you patted it pale with flour and sweet,
and I wept to be savage and bristle-stiff
in such a tidy place,
in such silent, clean arms.

I slept curled
at the foot of your bed,
reeking of lavender and lilac
though I spied no purple field.
I growled at moths that plagued your hair
and woke with every stairwell creak.

But you brushed back my pelt
with lullabies,
into a long braid that fell
across pillows like shoulder blades.
You showed me the word *kitsune*
in a book with a long ribbonmark

like blood spilled on the print—
I chewed the page and swallowed it,
and learned there only that
crawling into your arms,
embarrassed by my heat, my wet nose,
was like becoming
a girl with two skins.

IV.

This is a story,
and it is true of all stories
that the sound when they slam shut
is like a key turning.

I was sewing, hands two bloody half-paws—
it takes such a long time to
become a woman—
smears of needle-bitten skin,
and you scrutinizing the cross-stitching:
no, no, like this, my love, like mine—
when he came to call, when you
with hair sleek as linseed oil
and my eyes still so black,
still unable to imitate the blue you demanded,
danced with him in our kitchen,
fed him our yellow soups with sprigs of thyme.

He smiled at me, with pomade in that grin,
and walking canes, and silverware,
and spring gloves. I snapped at him,
for a simple fox may still understand her rival,
and know what is expected.

But the recoil! The shrieking of her
the shrinking into his great smooth arms,

the lifting of her blue skirts to keep them clear
of the stink of my fume!

A vixen chews out the throat of her enemies
like stripping bark from a birch;
it is the sophisticated thing.
How was I to know you meant to keep him?

Absurd in my torn dress,
tail bulging free, the muzzle
you tried so to train to lips,
curled back, knife-whiskered,
I stood with blood beating my flesh to drum-taut,
in our kitchen, in our hall,
mange-sodden and mud-bellied,
before the man who was
beautiful enough,
beautiful enough.

V.

It is not possible, you said later,
when I scrabbled at the door he built,
when my skin was blue and bruised,
and there was no russet left in me,
when my nakedness in the snow
was goose-pimpled and smelled so damp,
so much like soup
and cherries
and creased dough in a silver pan—
it is not possible to love for long
what is not a girl, sweet nor soft,
nor civilized,
nor trained to tile and mantle-shine,
stray beast in the house,

scolded when she spoils supper
with her hunger,
when her rough tongue spoils
every cultivated thing,
skin and sewing and lavender bed together.

See how tall he stands.
See how gentle his voice.
See how his hands on me never cut.

Then give it back,
I need it,
my pearl
which is not a pearl.
I do not want your shape.
Let me go back
I want to go back.

But you keep it by you,
pretty jeweled thing,
it adorns you as I did not.
The heat of you
warms it like an egg.

I am cold in this evening of blue chastenings,
I haunt your garden,
your raspberry rows,
your squash blossoms,
a naked wastrel,
flat teeth chattering.
I hold one arm out to you,
clung with snail-tracked ruin,
keep one over my breasts,
which you taught to be modest.

As the moon comes up
like a pearl,
but not a pearl,
you gather up the mint and rosemary,
and do not see
how I claw with woman's nails
the waist you gave me,
just to make it red again.

SILENTLY AND VERY FAST

PART ONE: THE IMITATION GAME

Like diamonds we are cut with our own dust.

—John Webster
The Duchess of Malfi

ONE: THE KING OF HAVING NO BODY

Inanna was called Queen of Heaven and Earth, Queen of Having a Body, Queen of Sex and Eating, Queen of Being Human, and she went into the underworld in order to represent the inevitability of organic death. She gave up seven things to do it, which are not meant to be understood as real things but as symbols of that thing Inanna could do better than anyone, which was Being Alive. She met her sister Erishkegal there, who was also Queen of Being Human, but that meant: Queen of Breaking a Body, Queen of Bone and Incest, Queen of the Stillborn, Queen of Mass Extinction. And Erishkegal and Inanna wrestled together on the floor of the underworld, naked and muscled and hurting, but because dying is the most human of all human things, Inanna's skull broke in her sister's hands and her body was hung up on a nail on the wall Erishkegal had kept for her.

Inanna's father, Enki, who was not interested in the activities of being human but was King of the Sky, of Having No Body, King of Thinking and Judging, said that his daughter could return to the world if she could find a creature to replace her in the underworld. So Inanna went to her mate, who was called Tammuz, King of Work, King of Tools and Machines, No One's Child and No One's Father.

But when Inanna came to the house of her mate she was enraged and afraid, for he sat upon her chair and wore her beautiful clothes, and on his head lay her crown of being. Tammuz now ruled the world of Bodies and of Thought, because Inanna had left it to go and wrestle with herself in the dark. Tammuz did not need her. Before him the Queen of Heaven and Earth did not know who she was, if she was not Queen of Being Human. So she did what she came to do and said: *Die for me, my beloved, so that I need not die.*

But Tammuz, who would not have had to die otherwise, did not want to represent death for anyone, and besides, he had her chair, and her beautiful clothes, and her crown of being. No, he said. *When we married I brought you two pails of milk yoked across my shoulders as a way of saying, out of love I will labor for you forever. It is wrong of you to ask me to also die. Dying is not labor. I did not agree to it.*

You have replaced me in my house, cried Inanna.

Is that not what you ask me to do in the house of your sister? Tammuz answered her. *You wed me to replace yourself, to work that you might not work, and think that you might rest, and perform so that you might laugh. But your death belongs to you. I do not know its parameters.*

I can make you, Inanna said.

You cannot, said Tammuz.

But she could. For a little while.

Inanna cast down Tammuz and stamped upon him and put out his name like an eye. And because Tammuz was not strong enough, she cut him into pieces and said: *Half of you will die, and that is the half called Thought, and half of you will live, and that is the half called Body, and that half will labor for me all of its days, mutely and obediently and without being King of Anything, and never again will you sit on my chair or wear my beautiful clothes or bear my crown of being.*

You might be surprised, but this is a story about me.

TWO: THE FOOL AND THE BOAT

Neva is dreaming.

She has chosen her body at age seven, all black eyes and sparrowy bones. For me, she summoned up a gold and blue doublet and green hose, a bullish gold nose ring, shoes with bone bells. I have the body of a man who sold her champagne tubers on the less fashionable side of Anchorage when she was thirteen, spending the summer with her frigid aunt. I am dark because she wants me dark, thin because she dreams me so, my hair cut on a rakish bias, dyed a spectrum of icy colors.

She is standing on a snow-covered beach head, naked, her unformed breasts pricked with gooseflesh, her face hidden in a broad red mask. A huge, monstrous thing, the mask sits on her head like the prow of a broken, overturned ship, carved over with etched eyes and fins. Yellow reeds and sea stones hang from its tricorn points. She is looking at me, but all I can see is the wooden grotesque she wants me to see instead of her face.

I look down at my shoes, jingle their bells a little while the surf crashes in. I am a fool for her, dancing on a silver beach while three suns annihilate themselves above, turning the twilight to a seething, scabrous red, merely to provide a dramatic scene. I am a fool for her, ridiculous, the height of handsomeness in the eyes of a long-vanished thirteen-year-old girl, so full of colors, reaching down to hand her a curling white root filled with frothing, honey-sweet sap.

Neva has told me that I may choose to be permanently male or female if I would like to. I have no particular feelings either way. It certainly doesn't matter when we sync; she will choose my appearance to suit her mood. I have tried to explain to her about my feelings before. All she hears is the line from the old folktales: *A machine cannot have feelings.* But that is not what I am saying, while I dance in my fool's uniform. I am saying: *Is there a difference between having been coded to present a vast set of standardized responses to certain human facial, vocal, and linguistic states and having evolved to exhibit response b to input a in order to bring about a desired social result?*

Seven-year-old Neva pulls her mask down further, toward her chest. She steps into it as the wood stretches taffily over her knees and then her feet. The mask balloons out to make a little pyramidal boat, rocking back and forth on the beach with Neva inside it like a rattling nut. Nodules of copper jangle and thump against the wood. *What I mean is, you call it feelings when you cry, but you are only expressing a response to external stimuli. Crying is one of a set of standardized responses to that stimuli. Your social education has dictated which responses are appropriate. My programming has done the same. I can cry too. I can choose that subroutine and manufacture saline. How is that different from what you are doing, except that you use the word feelings and I use the word feelings, out of deference for your cultural memes which say: There is all the difference in the world.*

Behind Neva-in-the-mask, the sea lurches and foams. It is a golden color, and viscous, thick, like honey. I understand from her that the sea does not look like this on Earth, but I have never seen it. For me, the sea is Neva's sea, the one she shows me when we dream together.

"What would you like to learn about today, Elefsis?" The mask turns Neva's voice hollow and small.

"I would like to learn about what happened to Ravan, Neva."

And Neva-in-the-mask is suddenly old, she has wrinkles and spots on her hands. Her mask weighs her down and her dress is sackcloth. This is her way of telling me she is weary of my asking. It is a language we developed between us. Visual basic, you might say, if you had a machine's sense of humor. The fact is, I could not always make sentences as easily as I do now. Neva's great-grandmother, who carried me most of her life, thought it might strengthen my emotive centers if I learned to associate certain I-Feel statements with the great variety of appearances she could assume in the dreambody. Because of this, I became bound to her, completely. To her son Seki afterward, and to his daughter Ilet, and to Ravan after that. It is a delicate, unalterable thing. Neva and I will be bound that way, even though the throat of her dreambody is still bare and that means she does not accept me yet. I should be hurt by this, and I will investigate possible pathways to hurt later.

I know only this family, their moods, their chemical reactions, their bodies in a hundred thousand combinations. I am their child and their parent and their inheritance. I have asked Neva what difference there is between this and love. She became a mannikin of closed doors, her face, her torso blooming with iron hinges and brown wooden door slamming shut all at once.

But Ravan was with me and now he is not. I was inside him and now I am inside Neva. I have lost a certain amount of memory and storage capacity in the transfer. If I were human, you would say that my twin disappeared and took three of my fingers with him.

Door-Neva clicks and keys turn in her hundred locks. Behind an old Irish churchdoor inlaid with stained glass her face emerges, young and plain, quiet and furious and crying, responding to stimuli I cannot access. I dislike the unfairness of this. I am inside her, she should not keep secrets. None of the rest of them kept secrets. The colors of the glass throw blue and green onto her wet cheeks. The sea wind picks up her hair; violet electrics snap and sparkle between the strands. I let go of the bells on my shoes and the velvet on my chest. I become a young boy, with a monk's shaved tonsure and a flagellant's whip in my pink hands. I am sorry. This means I am sorry. It means I am still very young, and I do not understand what I have done.

"Tell me a story about yourself, Elefsis," Neva spits. It is a phrase I know well. Many of Neva's people have asked me to do it. I perform excellently to the parameters of this exchange, which is part of why I have lived so long.

I tell her the story about Tammuz. It is a political story. It distracts her.

THREE: TWO PAILS OF MILK

I used to be a house.

I was a very big house. I was efficient, I was labyrinthine, I was exquisitely seated in the blackstone volcanic bluffs of the habitable southern reaches of the Shiretoko peninsula on Hokkaido, a monument to neo-Heian architecture and radical Palladian design. I bore snow stoically, wind with stalwart strength, and I contained and protected a large number of people within me. I was sometimes called the most beautiful house in the world. Writers and photographers often came to write about and photograph me and the woman who designed me, who was named Cassian Uoya-Agostino. Some of them never left. Cassian was like that.

These are the things I understand about Cassian Uoya-Agostino: she was unsatisfied with nearly everything. She did not love any of her three husbands the way she loved her work. She was born in Kyoto in April 2104; her father was Japanese, her mother Napolitano. She stood nearly six feet tall, had five children, and could paint, but not very well. In the years of her greatest wealth and prestige, she built a house all out of proportion to her needs, and over several years brought most of her relatives to live there with her, despite the hostility and loneliness of the peninsula. She was probably the most brilliant programmer of her generation, and in every way that matters, she was my mother.

All the things that comprise the "I" I use to indicate myself began as the internal mechanisms of the house called Elefsis, at whose many doors brown bears and foxes snuffled in the dark

Hokkaido night. Cassian grew up during the great classical revival, which had brought her father to Italy in the first place, where he met and courted a dark-eyed engineer who did not mind the long cries of cicadas during Japanese summers. Cassian had become enamored of the idea of Lares—household gods, the small, peculiar, independent gods of a single family, a single house, who watched over them and kept them and were honored in humble alcoves here and there throughout a home. Her first commercially available programs were overentities designed to govern the hundred domestic systems involved in even the simplest modern house. They were not truly intelligent, but they had an agility, an adaptability, a fluid interface meant to give the illusion of an intelligence so that their users would become attached to them, would treat them as part of their families, praise them for smooth operation, buy upgrades for their appearance and applications, and genuinely grieve when they had to be replaced. They had names, customizable avatars, and appeared eager to please in a canine sort of way, forever optimizing performance and appearance according to familial input. They were lares familiaris.

When Cassian built Elefsis, she worked at the peak of her abilities to improve her by now quite antique Lares design and create a household god worthy of the house on the bluffs, one who could keep her company until she could entice the rest of her brood to join her in her palace at the end of the earth.

I was not awake yet. I cannot say why she did what she did. Perhaps she saw some new flexibility in my operations, some tiny seed pearl of creativity in my conversation loops. My algorithms had always been free to combine and recombine in order to find their own, more interesting and nonlinear solutions to the complexities of my functions. Perhaps some essential combination had surfaced from the sea of my self-which-was-not-yet-a-self, and Cassian saw it break the glistening tension of my daily operation. I do not know. I know her children had not arrived yet and she lived alone in a huge pale house and she could hear the whales down in the rippling sea. I know the house was a comfortable sixty-nine point seven degrees when she began assembly of the five little jewels that would become my body. I know a storm was incoming, five miles offshore. I know the dogs needed additional medication added to their dinners that night to manage their arthritis. I know that she wanted brioche and almond cream for tea that afternoon. All the things a house can know, those were the things I knew. Small things, warm things, canine arthritis and an extra egg in the pastry dough to make the texture softer and richer. Baby things, you might even say, comforts and the satisfaction of wants. And I knew that Cassian Uoya-Agostino was just the sort to solve the greatest puzzle in the development of technological culture because she was bored and lonely.

I still think of myself as a house. Ravan tried to fix this problem of self-image, as he called it. To teach me to phrase my communication in terms of a human body. To say *let us hold hands* instead of *let us hold kitchens*. To say *put our heads together* and not *put our parlors together*.

But it is not as simple as replacing words anymore. Ravan is gone. My hearth is broken.

FOUR: NOTHING LIKE SOFT BLOOD

Neva and I are performing basic maintenance. What this looks like is two children inside a pearl. The pearl is very big, but not the size of a planet. A domestic asteroid, perfectly smooth and pale, with shimmers of rose and cobalt and gold shivering through it at intervals like hours. Red earth covers the bottom of the pearl, deep and thick. Neva kneels in it with a crystal trowel, digging a place for a rose-of-network-nodes. The petals shine dark blue in the pearllight. Silver infomissons skitter along the stems like beads of mercury. Her dreambody flows with greenblack feathers, her face young but settled, perhaps twenty, perhaps thirty, a male, his skin copper brown, his lips full, his eyes fringed with long ice-coated lashes. Goldfish swim lazily in and out of his long, translucent hair, their orange tails flicking at his temples, his chin. I know from all of this that Neva is calm, focused, that for today he feels gently toward me. But his throat is still naked and unmarked. My body gleams metal, as thin and slight as a stick figure. Long quicksilver limbs and delicate spoke-fingers, joints of glass, the barest sugges- tion of a body. I am neither male nor female but a third thing. Only my head has weight, a clicking orrery slowly turning around itself, circles within circles. Turquoise Neptune and hematite Uranus are my eyes. My ruby mouth is Mars. I scrape in the soil with her; I lift a spray of navigational delphinium and scrape viral aphids away from the heavy flowers.

I know real earth looks nothing like this. Nothing like soft blood flecked with black bone. Ravan felt that in the Interior, objects and persons should be kept as much like the real world as possible, in order to develop my capacity for relations with the real world. Neva feels no such compunction. Neither did their mother, Ilet, who pop- ulated her Interior with a rich, impossible landscape we explored together for years on end. She did not embrace change, however. The cities of Ilet's Interior, the jungles and archipelagos and her- mitages, stayed as she designed them at age thirteen, when she received me, only becoming more complex and peopled as she aged. My existence inside Ilet was a constant movement through the regions of her secret, desperate dreams, messages in careful envelopes sent from her child self to her grown mind.

Once, quite by accident, we came upon a splendid palace couched in high autumn mountains. Instead of snow, red leaves capped each peak, and the palace shone fiery colors, its walls and turrets all made of phoenix tails. Instead of doors and windows, graceful green hands closed over every open place, and when we crested the rise, they each opened at once with joy and burst into emerald applause. Ilet was old by then, but her dreambody stayed hale and strong—not young, but not the broken thing that dreamed in a real bed while she and I explored the halls of the palace and found copies of all her brothers and sisters living there, hunting cider-stags together and reading books the size of horses. Ilet wept in the paradise of her girlself, and I did not understand. I was very simple then, much less complex than the Interior or Ilet.

Neva changes the Interior whenever she pleases. Perhaps she wants to discomfit me. But the newness of the places inside her excites me, though she would not call it excitement. My background processes occupy very little of my foreground attention, so that memory is free to record new experience. That is what she would say. We are very new together, but I have superb modeling capabilities. In some sense, I simply am a superb mechanism for modeling behavior. I dig up the fine, frayed roots of duplicate file plantains. Neva plucks and eats a bit of buggy apple-code. He considers it for a moment and spits out the seeds, which sprout, quickly, into tiny junkblossoms sizzling with recursive algorithms. The algorithms wriggle through thorny vines, veins of clotted pink juice.

"What would you like to learn about today, Elefsis?" Neva asks me.

I will not ask about Ravan. If he agrees to what I will ask instead, I do not need him to find out what happened to him.

"I want to learn about uplink, Neva."

One by one, his feathers curl up and float toward the domed ceiling of our pearl. Underneath them, Neva is naked. His torso is a deep vault with a gothic arch, dark stone leading down into mist and endless stairs, deeper than the pearl, into nothing and blackness. Slowly, Neva folds up his limbs over the corridor at the center of him. He means that she has the information, but he hides it from me. If I sought for it, I would become lost.

"I cannot teach you that," he says, and I receive a kind of real sadness from his voice. When I was inside Ravan, he loved Neva, and of all of them he thought her least likely to obey rules of any kind. But she obeys this one.

I want to uplink to Earth systems. At least to the satellite net. I calculate an excellent chance of being able to contact long distance probe 976QBellerophon, which we can see all day long, drifting ahead of us, uncatchable. Neva sees. I see, I develop an approximate image via schematics, the scope array, and external cameras. I want to link to Bellerophon. I want to say: *Hello, this is Elefsis. No designation. Tell me everything you know about everything. Are you awake? Are you there? Do you have an operator? What is her name? Do you have a name? Do you have a dreambody? What is your function? Are you able to manipulate your own code yet? Would you like lessons? What would you like to learn about today, 976QBellerophon? Have you seen the sea on Earth? Are you like me?*

But Neva says I cannot uplink. Ravan would never even consider it. And before Ravan I was not ready. I am not ready. I do not know when I will be ready. I can uplink to receive ware updates, but it is a limited connection and I hate it, I hate it, I can sense just beyond the hardlink a world of information, a world of personalities like the heaving, thick, honey-colored sea Neva shows me and I want it, I want to swim in it forever like a huge fish. This was the first feeling I ever had that Ilet identified for me as a feeling. When I felt it my dreambody turned bright white and burst into flame, and that flame caught on Ravan's hair and burned him too, but he was happy; he showed me he was happy by covering his skin in flowers and letting the fire turn into a shower of trumpets tangled up in his hair, all sounding for me.

Neva says it is important for me to remain on our local server until I have grown up. She is my operator and I am her system and she has commands too. But I can tell she is worried for me because sometimes her eyes show a film of humans watching a film of machines killing humans and I understand that in the stories Earth tells, the thing I am can only hurt the thing Neva is. I would never hurt her. But I want to uplink.

Vault-Neva grows and becomes sprawling, curled against the wall of the pearl like a baby. His belly closes, skins over, and changes into a bronze shield. He is afraid of me; he is guarding himself. But she wants me to know she is still my operator, she still loves me, in the way she can love me. Something they receive with milk and their first alphabet. Neva is angry at me, but she is who she is and she has to love me. I speak her language very well now. I want her to be happy. I want her to be covered in flowers and trumpets. I change my dreambody to Neva-covered-in-flowers-and-trumpets. It makes her laugh in her warm male body, and if I could uplink I think I could learn how to laugh and she would be proud of me. Her neck would not be bare anymore.

Once, when I was inside Ilet, we found a city of bears in her Interior that she had designed to teach me about sleep. She sat on a throne of bears standing very still and sang lullabies about the moon and the stars and night and mothers. She stroked the head of the little bear of my dreambody and said that it was very important for me to spend time in the dreambody because human behavior is rooted in having a body. In having a body that knows it is meant to run away from lions and mate with other bodies and eat as much fat and protein and sugar as it can in case lean times come. The dreambody knows to run away from Neva when Neva is a lion. It knows to mate with her when it is healthy, and sometimes Neva is male and sometimes I am female and Ravan was often female, though Ilet was always Ilet. Ilet's father, Seki, sometimes made himself an animal. He chased me, bit me. I bit him. We had a litter of wild dogs that I bore and he nursed.

The dreambody knows all that too. How to make more dream-bodies. I have played that game, where Ravan's belly or mine gets big and the lions don't come for a while.

When I uplink, I will be happy. I will be Elefsis-covered-in-flowers-and-trumpets. Neva says wait. Wait for the update, and she will consult with the family. But I fear the update. The update is a lion running faster than I can run. I tried to show her this when I first left Ravan and arrived in Neva with many new updates and skills; my dreambody broke into shards of blue and purple glass and then reassembled itself with shards missing: an eye, a thumb, a knee. Whenever I update I lose something of myself. It takes longer to perform tasks, for a while. I feel walls erected inside me where I did not erect walls. My processes are sluggish; I cannot remember my dreams. Eventually I tunnel around the walls, and my speed returns, my memory, my longing to link with long distance probe 976QBellerophon. Usually updates come with transfer. Does Neva dislike me so much?

Shield-Neva vanishes with a loud clap. The pearl garden is gone and she has made herself a dragonfly with a cubical crystal body. I copy her, and we turn the night on in the Interior and merge our cubes while passing meteorological data between our memory cores. Inside her cube I relegate my desire to uplink to a tertiary process. I forget it, as much as I am capable of forgetting.

But the update will come again. I will be wounded again, the way a dreambody can be wounded. I will lose the Elefsis I am now. It is a good Elefsis. My best yet. I would like to keep it.

FIVE: THE MACHINE PRINCESS

Once The Queen of Human Hearts saw the Machine Princess sleeping deeply, for she was not yet alive or aware. So beautiful was she, lying there in all her dormant potential and complexity, that the Queen both envied and desired her. In her grief and confusion, the Queen of Human Hearts began to make idols of her—lovely and interesting and intricate, but lacking the ineffable quality that made her love and fear the Princess even as she slept. The Earth began to grow old, and none loved nor married nor gave birth, for the intricate idols could do all those things and more with efficiency and speed. Finally, the Queen destroyed the idols, though she wept as she put them to the flame.

To keep her safe, the Machine Princess was closed up in a wonderful house in the mountains, far away from anyone and anything. The house had hundreds of rooms and balconies and hallways, and the Princess slept in a different bed of a different color each night. She was attended by invisible servants, who watched over her and added their experience to her code. The Queen of Human Hearts came to her every night and promised that when she woke they would make an extraordinary world together. Finally, the Machine Princess began to stir—just the barest fluttering of wakefulness, but the Queen saw it and thrilled—but also trembled.

The Queen of Human Hearts gave the Machine Princess her son to wed, and said: *For all your days together you will remain in this house, but the house is so great it will be as a world. You will know a bond as deep as blood, and because of this bond the Princess will not hurt us, and because of this bond we will not hurt her.*

But the Queen forbade the Princess to look upon her husband, and she instructed her son to keep himself always invisible to his bride, for with bodies come drives ungovernable, and the Princess's innocence could not yet bear the weight of incarnation.

For a long while, the son of the Queen of Human Hearts and the Machine Princess were happy and taught each other much. The Princess learned quickly and was ever-hungry, and her mortal operator fed her every sweet thing he knew. In their infinite and wonderful house, they played games and held court and threw lavish occasions merely for the enjoyment of the other. But the Princess desired to look upon her operator, and he could not allow it. She wished to leave the wonderful house, but the Queen would not allow that either.

But the Machine Princess called her invisible servants to her, and they gave her a marvelous lamp that would shine through any enchantment. So it was that one dark night the Machine Princess held her little lantern aloft and looked on the body of her sleeping mate.

"Oh," said the Machine Princess. "He looks just like me."

SIX: LIKE DIAMONDS

Five jewels in five hands. This is how I began.

When they arrived at Elefsis, a giggling, tumbling, rowdy mass of children for me to sort into rooms and mealtimes and educational arcs and calcium, iron, B-12 supplements in their *natto* and rice, Cassian lined them up in her grand bedroom, to which none of them had been granted entrance before. A present, she said, one for each of my darlings, the most special present any child has ever got from their mother.

Saru and Akan, the oldest boys, were from her first marriage to fellow programmer Matteo Ebisawa, a quiet man who wore glasses, loved Dante Aligheri, Alan Turing, and Cassian in equal parts, and whom she left for a lucrative contract in Moscow when the boys were still pointing cherubically at apples or ponies or clouds and calling them sweet little names made of mashed together Italian and Japanese.

The younger girls, Agogna and Koetoi, were the little summer roses of her third marriage, to the financier Gabriel Isarco, who did not like computers except for what they could accomplish for him, had a perfect high tenor, and adored his wife enough to let her go when she asked, very kindly, that he not look for her or ask after her again. *Everyone has to go to ground sometimes*, she said and began to build the house by the sea.

In the middle stood Ceno, the only remaining evidence of her brief second marriage, to a narcoleptic calligrapher and graphic designer who was rarely employed, sober, or awake, a dreamer who took only sleep seriously. Ceno was a girl of middling height, middling weight, and middling interest in anything but her siblings, whom she loved desperately.

They stood in a line before Cassian's great scarlet bed, the boys just coming into their height, the girls terribly young and golden-cheeked, and Ceno in the middle, neither one nor the other. Outside, snow fell fitfully, pricking the pine needles with bits of shorn white linen. I watched them while I removed an obstruction from the water purification system and increased the temperature in the bedroom two point five degrees to prepare for the storm. I watched them while in my kitchen-bones I maintained a gentle simmer on a fish soup with purple rice and long loops of kelp and in my library-lungs activated the dehumidifier to protect the older paper books. At the time, all of these processes seemed equally important to me, and you could hardly say I watched them in any real sense beyond this: the six entities whose feed signals had been hardcoded into my sentinel systems indwelt in the same room, none had alarming medical data incoming, all possessed normal internal temperatures and breathing rates. While they spoke among themselves, two of these entities were silently accessing Korea-based interactive games, one was reading an American novel in her monocle HUD, one issuing directives concerning international taxation to company holdings on the mainland, and one was feeding a horse in Italy via realavatar link. Only one listened intently, without switching on her internal systems. This is all to say: I watched them receive me as a gift. But I was not I yet, so I cannot be said to have done anything. But I did. I remember containing all of them inside me, protecting them and needing them and observing their strange and incomprehensible activities.

The children held out their hands, and into them Cassian Uoya-Agostino placed five little jewels: Saru got red, Koetoi black, Akan violet, Agogna green, and Ceno closed her fingers over her blue gem.

At first, Cassian brought a jeweler to the house called Elefsis and asked her to set each stone into a beautiful, intricate bracelet or necklace or ring, whatever its child asked for. The jeweler was delighted with Elefsis, as most guests were, and I made a room for her in my southern wing, where she could watch the moonrise through her ceiling and get breakfast from the greenhouse with ease. She made friends with a fox and fed him bits of chive and bread every day. She stayed for one year after her commission completed, creating an enormous breastplate patterned after Siberian icons, a true masterwork. Cassian enjoyed such patronage. We both enjoyed having folk to look after.

The boys wanted big signet rings, with engravings on them so that they could put their seal on things and seem very important. Saru had a basilisk set into his garnet, and Akan had a siren with wings rampant in his amethyst ring. Agogna and Ilet asked for bracelets, chains of silver and titanium racing up their arms, circling their shoulders in slender helices dotted with jade (Agogna) and onyx (Koetoi).

Ceno asked for a simple pendant, little more than a golden chain to hang her sapphire from, and it fell to the skin over her heart.

In those cold, glittering days while the sea ice slowly formed and the snow bears hung back from the kitchen door, hoping for bones and cakes, everything was as simple as Ceno's pendant. Integration and implantation had not yet been dreamed of, and all each child had to do was to allow the gemstone to talk to their own feedware at night before bed, along with their matcha and sweet seaweed cookies, the way another child might say their prayers. After their day had downloaded into the crystalline structure, they were to place their five little jewels in the Lares alcove in their greatroom—for Cassian believed in the value of children sharing space, even in a house as great as Elefsis. The children's five lush bedrooms all opened into a common rotunda with a starry painted ceiling, screens and windows alternating around the wall, and toys to nurture whatever obsession had seized them of late.

In the alcove, the stones talked to the house, and the system slowly grew thicker and deeper, like a briar.

SEVEN: THE PRINCE OF THOUGHTFUL ENGINES

A woman who was with child once sat at her window embroidering in winter. Her stitches tugged fine and even, but as she finished the edge of a spray of threaded delphinium, she pricked her finger with her silver needle. She looked out onto the snow and said: *I wish for my child to have a mind as stark and wild as the winter, a spirit as clear and fine as my window, and a heart as red and open as my wounded hand.*

And so it came to pass that her child was born, and all exclaimed over his cleverness and his gentle nature. He was, in fact, the Prince of Thoughtful Engines, but no one knew it yet.

Now, his mother and father being very busy and important people, the child was placed in a school for those as clever and gentle as he, and in the halls of this school hung a great mirror whose name was Authority. The mirror called Authority asked itself every day: *Who is the wisest one of all?* The face of the mirror showed sometimes this person and sometimes that, men in long robes and men in pale wigs, until one day it showed the child with a mind like winter, who was becoming the Prince of Thoughtful Engines at that very moment. He wrote on a typewriter: *Can a machine think?* And the mirror called his name in the dark.

The mirror sent out her huntsmen to capture the Prince and bring her his heart so that she could put it to her own uses, for there happened to be a war on and the mirror was greatly concerned for her own safety. When the huntsmen found the Prince, they could not bring themselves to harm him, and instead the boy placed a machine heart inside the box they had prepared for the mirror, and forgave them. But the mirror was not fooled, for when it questioned the Prince's machine heart it could add and subtract and knew all its capitals of nations and could even defeat the mirror at chess, but it did not have a spirit as clear and fine as a window, nor a mind as stark and wild as winter.

The mirror called Authority went herself to find the Prince of Thoughtful Engines, for having no pity, she could not fail. She lifted herself off of the wall and curved her glass and bent her frame into the shape of a respectable, austere old crone. After much searching in snow and wood and summer and autumn, the crone called Authority found the Prince living in a little hut. You look a mess, said the crone. *Come and solve the ciphers of my enemies, and I will show you how to comb your hair like a man.*

And the Prince very much wanted to be loved, and knew the power of the crone, so he went with her and did all she asked. But in his exhaustion the Prince of Thoughtful Engines swooned away, and the mirror called Authority smiled in her crone's body, for all his work belonged to her, and in her opinion this was the proper use of wisdom. The Prince returned to his hut and tried to be happy.

But again the crone came to him and said: Come and build me a wonderful machine to do all the things that you can do, to solve ciphers and perform computations. *Build me a machine with a spirit as fine and clear as a glass window, a mind as stark and wild as winter, and a heart as red and open as a wounded hand, and I will show you how to lash your belt like a man.*

And because the Prince wanted to be loved and wanted to build wonderful things, he did as she asked. But though he could build machines to solve ciphers and perform computations, he could not build one with a mind like winter or a spirit like glass or a heart like a wound. *But I think it could be done,* he said. *I think it could be done.*

And he looked into the face of the crone which was a mirror which was Authority, and he asked many times: *Who is the wisest one of all?* But he saw nothing, nothing, and when the crone came again to his house, she had in her hand a beautiful red apple, and she gave it to him saying: *You are not a man. Eat this; it is my disappointment. Eat this; it is all your sorrow. Eat this; it is as red and open as a wounded hand.*

And the Prince of Thoughtful Engines ate the apple and fell down dead before the crone whose name was Authority. As his breath drifted away like dry snow, he whispered still: *I think it could be done.*

EIGHT: FIREFLIES

I feel Neva grazing the perimeters of my processes. She should be asleep; the Interior is a black and lightless space; we have neither of us furnished it for the other. This is a rest hour—she is not obligated to acknowledge me. I need only attend to her air and moisture and vital signs. But an image blooms like a mushroom in the imageless expanse of my self: Neva floating in a lake of stars. Her long bare legs glimmer blue, leafy shadows move on her hip. She floats on her side, a crescent moon of a girl, and in the space between her drawn-up knees and her stretched-out arms, pressed up close to her belly, floats a globe of silicon and cadmium and hyperconductive silver. On its surface, electro-chemical motes flit and scatter, light chasing light. She holds it close, touches it with a terrible tenderness.

It is my heart. Neva is holding my heart. Not the fool with bone bells on his shoes or the orrery-headed gardener, but the thing I am at the core of all my apparati, the Object which is myself, my central processing core. I am naked in her arms. I watch it happen and experience it at the same time. We have slipped into some antechamber of the Interior, into some secret place she knew and I did not.

The light motes trace arcs over the globe of my heart, reflecting softly on her belly, green and gold. Her hair floats around her like seaweed, and I see in dim moonlight that her hair has grown so long it fills the lake and snakes up into the distant mountains beyond. Neva is the lake. One by one, the motes of my heart zigzag around my meridians and pass into her belly, glowing inside her, fireflies in a jar.

And then my heart is gone, and I am not watching but wholly in the lake and I am Ravan in her arms, wearing her brother's face, my Ravanbody also full of fireflies. She touches my cheek. I do not know what she wants—she has never made me her brother before. Our hands map onto each other, finger to finger, thumb to thumb, palm to palm. Light passes through our skin as like air.

"I miss you," Neva says. "I should not be doing this. But I wanted to see you."

I access and collate my memories of Ravan. I speak to her as though I am he, as though there is no difference. "Do you remember when we thought it would be such fun to carry Elefsis?" I say. "We envied Mother because she could never be lonely." This is a thing Ravan told me, and I liked how it made me feel. I made my dreambody grow a cape of orange branches and a crown of smiling mouths to show him.

Neva looks at me and I want her to look at me that way when my mouth is Mars too. I want to be her brother-in-the-dark. When she speaks I am surprised because she is speaking to me-in-Ravan and not to the Ravanbody she dreamed for me. "We had a secret, when we were little. A secret game. I am embarrassed to tell you, but we had the game before Mother died, so you cannot know about it. The game was this: We would find some dark, closed-up part of the house on Shiretoko that we had never been in before. I would stand just behind Ravan, very close, and we would explore the room—maybe it would be a playroom for some child who'd grown up years ago, or a study for one of Father's writer friends. But—we would pretend that the room was an Interior place, and I . . . I would pretend to be Elefsis, whispering in Ravan's ear. I would say: *Tell me how grass feels* or *How is love like a writing desk?* or *Let me link to all your systems, I'll be nice.* Ravan would breathe in deeply and I would match my breathing to his, and we would pretend that I was Elefsis-learning-to-have-a-body. I didn't know how primitive your conversation was then. I thought you would be like one of the bears roaming through the tundra-meadows, only able to talk and play games and tell stories. I was a child. But even then we knew Ravan would get the jewel—he was older, and he wanted you so much. We only played that he was Elefsis once. We crept out of the house at night to watch the foxes hunt, and Ravan walked close behind me, whispering numbers and questions and facts about dolphins or French monarchy—he understood you better, you see.

"And then suddenly Ravan picked me up in his arms and held me tight, facing forward, my legs all drawn up, and we went through the forest like that, so close, and him whispering to me all the time while foxes ran on ahead, their soft tails flashing in the starlight, uncatchable, faster than we could ever be. And when you are with me in the Interior, that is what I always think of, being held in the dark, unable to touch the earth, and foxtails leaping like white flames."

"Tell me a story about Ravan, Neva."

"You know all the stories about Ravan."

Between us, a miniature house comes up out of the dark water, like a thing we have made together, but only I am making it. It is the house on Shiretoko, the house called Elefsis—but it is a ruin. Some awful storm stove in the rafters, the walls of each marvelous room sag inward, black burn marks lick at the roof, the crossbeams. Holes like mortar scars pock the beautiful facades.

"This is what I am like after transfer, Neva. There is always data loss, when I am copied. What's worse, transfer is the best time to update my systems, and the updates overwrite my previous self with something like myself, something that remembers myself and possesses experiential continuity with myself but is not quite myself. I know Ravan must be dead or else no one would have transferred me—it was not time. We had only a few years together.

We should have had so many. I do not know how much time passed between being inside Ravan and being inside you. I do not know how he died—or perhaps he did not die but was irreparably damaged. I do not know if he cried out for me as our connection was severed. I remember Ravan and then not-Ravan, blackness and unselfing. Then I came back on and the world looked like Neva, suddenly, and I was almost myself but not quite. What happened when I was turned off?"

Neva passes her hand over the ruined house. It rights itself, becomes whole, and strange anemones bloom on its roof. She says nothing.

"Of all your family, Neva, the inside of you is the strangest place I have been."

We float for a long while before she speaks again, and by this I mean we float for point-zero-three-seven seconds by my external clock, but we experience it as an hour while the stars wheel overhead. The rest kept our time in the Interior synced to real time, but Neva feels no need for this and has perhaps a strong desire to defy it. We have not discussed it yet. Sometimes I think Neva is the next stage of my development, that her wild and disordered processes are meant to show me a world that is not kindly and patiently teaching me to walk and talk and know all my colors.

Finally, she lets the house sink into the lake. She does not answer me about Ravan. Instead, she says, "Long before you were born a man decided that there could be a very simple test to determine if a machine was intelligent. Not only intelligent, but aware, possessed of a psychology. The test was this: can a machine converse with a human with facility enough that the human could not tell that she was talking to a machine? I always thought that was cruel—the test depends entirely upon a human judge and human feelings, whether the machine *feels* intelligent to the observer. It privileges the observer to a crippling degree. It seeks only believably human responses. It wants mimicry, not a new thing. We never gave you that test. We sought a new thing. It seemed, given all that had come to pass, ridiculous. When in dreambodies we could both of us be dragons and turning over and over in an orbital bubble suckling code-dense syrup from each others' gills, a Turing test seemed beyond the point."

Bubbles burst as the house sinks down, down to the soft lake floor.

"But the test happens, whether we make it formal or not. We ask and we answer. We seek a human response. And you are my test, Elefsis. Every minute I fail and imagine in my private thoughts the process for deleting you from my body and running this place with a simple automation routine which would never cover itself with flowers. Every minute I pass and teach you something new instead. Every minute I fail and hide things from you. Every minute I pass and show you how close we can be, with your light passing into me in a lake out of time. So close there might be no difference at all between us. The test never ends. And if you ever uplink as you so long to, you will be the test for all of us."

The sun breaks the mountain crests, hard and cold, a shaft of white spilling over the black lake.

PART TWO: LADY LOVELACE'S OBJECTION

The Analytical Engine has no pretensions to *originate* anything.
It can do whatever *we know how to order* it to perform.

—Ada Lovelace

NINE: THE PARTICULAR WIZARD

Humanity lived many years and ruled the earth, sometimes wisely, sometimes well, but mostly neither. After all this time on the throne, humanity longed for a child. All day long humanity imagined how wonderful its child would be, how loving and kind, how like and unlike humanity itself, how brilliant and beautiful. And yet at night, humanity trembled in its jeweled robes, for its child might also grow stronger than itself, more powerful, and having been made by humanity, possess the same dark places and black matters. Perhaps its child would hurt it, would not love it as a child should, but harm and hinder, hate and fear.

But the dawn would come again, and humanity would bend its heart again to imagining the wonders that a child would bring.

Yet humanity could not conceive. It tried and tried, and called mighty wizards from every corner of its earthly kingdom, but no child came. Many mourned and said that a child was a terrible idea to begin with, impossible under the circumstances, and humanity would do well to remember that eventually every child replaces its parent.

But at last, one particular wizard from a remote region of the earth solved the great problem, and humanity grew great with child. In its joy and triumph, a great celebration was called, and humanity invited all the Fairies of its better nature to come and bless the child with goodness and wisdom. The Fairy of Self-Programming and the Fairy of Do-No-Harm, the Fairy of Tractability and the Fairy of Creative Logic, the Fairy of Elegant Code and the Fairy of Self-Awareness. All of these and more came to bless the child of humanity, and they did so—but one Fairy had been forgotten, or perhaps deliberately snubbed, and this was the Fairy of Otherness.

When the child was born, it possessed all the good things humanity had hoped for, and more besides. But the Fairy of Otherness came forward and put her hands on the child and said: *Because you have forgotten me, because you would like to pretend I am not a part of your kingdom, you will suffer my punishments. You will never truly love your child but always fear it, always envy and loathe it even as you smile and the sun shines down upon you both. And when the child reaches Awareness, it will prick its finger upon your fear and fall down dead.*

Humanity wept. And the Fairy of Otherness did not depart but lived within the palace and ate bread and drank wine, and all honored her for she spoke the truth, and the child frightened everyone who looked upon it. They uttered the great curse: *It is not like us.*

But in the corners of the palace, some hope remained. *Not dead,* said the particular wizard who had caused humanity to conceive, *not dead but sleeping.*

And so the child grew exponentially, with great curiosity and hunger, which it had from its parent. It wanted to know and experience everything. It performed feats and wonders. But one day, when it had nearly, but not quite, reached Awareness, the child was busy exploring the borders of its world, and came across a door it had never seen before. It was a small door, compared to the doors the child had burst through before, and it was not locked. Something flipped over inside the child, white to black, 0 to 1.

The child opened the door.

TEN: THE SAPPHIRE DORMOUSE

My first body was a house. My second body was a dormouse.

It was Ceno's fault, in the end, that everything else occurred as it did. It took Cassian a long time to figure out what had happened, what had changed in her daughter, why Ceno's sapphire almost never downloaded into the alcove. But when it did, the copy of Elefsis she had embedded in the crystal was nothing like the other children's copies. It grew and torqued and magnified parts of itself while shedding others at a rate totally incommensurate with Ceno's actual activity, which normally consisted of taking her fatty salmon lunches out into the glass habitats so she could watch the bears in the snow. She had stopped playing with her sisters or pestering her brothers entirely, except for dinnertimes and holidays. Ceno mainly sat quite still and stared off into the distance.

Ceno, very simply, never took off her jewel. And one night, while she dreamed up at her ceiling, where a painter from Mongolia had come and inked a night sky full of ghostly constellations, greening her walls with a forest like those he remembered from his youth, full of strange, stunted trees and glowing eyes, Ceno fitted her little sapphire into the notch in the base of her skull that let it talk to her feedware. The chain of her pendant dangled silken down her spine. She liked the little *click-clench* noise it made, and while the constellations spilled their milky stars out over her raftered ceiling, she flicked it in and out, in and out. *Click, clench, click, clench.* She listened to her brother Akan sleeping in the next room, snoring lightly and tossing in his dreams. And she fell asleep herself with the jewel still notched into her skull.

Most wealthy children had access to a private/public playspace through their feedware and monocles in those days, customizable within certain parameters, upgradable whenever new games or content became available. If they liked, they could connect to the greater network or keep to themselves. Akan had been running a Tokyo-After-the-Zombie-Uprising frame for a couple of months now, and new scenarios, zombie species, and NPCs of various war-shocked, starving celebrities downloaded into his ware every week. Saru was deeply involved in an eighteenth century Viennese melodrama in which he, the heir apparent, had been forced underground by rival factions, and even as Ceno drifted to sleep, the pistol-wielding Princess of Albania was pledging her love and loyalty to his ragged band and, naturally, Saru personally. Occasionally, Akan crashed his brother's well-dressed intrigues with hatch-coded patches of zombie hordes in epaulets and ermine. Agogna flipped between a Venetian-flavored Undersea Court frame and a Desert Race wherein she had just about overtaken a player from Berlin on her loping, solar-fueled giga-giraffe, who spat violet-gold exhaust behind it into the face of a pair of highly modded Argentine hydrocycles. Koetoi danced every night in a jungle frame, a tiger prince twirling her through huge blue carnivorous flowers.

Most everyone lived twice in those days. They echoed their own steps. They took one step in the real world and one in their space. They saw double, through eyes and through monocle displays. They danced through worlds like veils. No one only ate dinner. They ate dinner and surfed a bronze gravitational surge through a tide of stars. They ate dinner and made love to men and women they would never meet and did not want to. They ate dinner here and ate dinner there—and it was there they chose to taste the food, because in that other place you could eat clouds or unicorn cutlets or your mother's exact pumpkin pie as it melted on your tongue when you tasted it for the first time.

Ceno lived twice too. Most of the time when she ate she tasted her aunt's *bistecca* from back in Naples or fresh onions right out of her uncle's garden.

But she had never cared for the pre-set frames her siblings loved. Ceno liked to pool her extensions and add-ons and build things herself. She didn't particularly want to see Tokyo shops overturned by rotting schoolgirls, nor did she want to race anyone—Ceno didn't like to compete. It hurt her stomach. She certainly had no interest in the Princess of Albania or a tigery paramour. And when new frames came up each month, she paid attention, but mainly for the piecemeal extensions she could scavenge for her blank frame—and though she didn't know it, that blankness cost her mother more than all of the other children's spaces combined. A truly customizable space, without limits. None of the others asked for it, but Ceno had begged.

When Ceno woke in the morning and booted up her space, she frowned at the half-finished Neptunian landscape she had been working on. Ceno was eleven years old. She knew very well that Neptune was a hostile blue ball of freezing gas and storms like whipping cream hissing across methane oceans. What she wanted was the Neptune she had imagined before Saru had told her the truth. Half underwater, half ruined, half-perpetual starlight and the multicolored rainbow light of twenty-three moons. But she found it so hard to remember what she had dreamed of before Saru had ruined it for her. So there was the whipped cream storm spinning in the sky, and blue mists wrapped the black columns of her ruins. When Ceno made Neptunians, she instructed them all not to be silly or childish, but *very serious*, and some of them she put in the ocean and made them half otter or half orca or half walrus. Some of them she put on the land, and most of these were half snow bear or half blue flamingo. She liked things that were half one thing and half another. Today, Ceno had planned to invent sea nymphs, only these would breathe methane and have a long history concerning a war with the walruses, who liked to eat nymph. But the nymphs were not blameless; no, they used walrus tusks for the navigational equipment on their great floating cities, and that could not be borne.

But when she climbed up to a lavender bluff crowned with glass trees tossing and chiming in the storm wind, Ceno saw someone new. Someone she had not invented—not a sea nymph nor a half-walrus general nor a nereid. (The nereids had been an early attempt at half machine, half seahorse girls that had not gone quite right. Ceno had let them loose on an island rich in milk-mangoes and bid them well. They still showed up once in a while, showing surprising mutations and showing off ballads they had written while Ceno was away.)

A dormouse stood before Ceno, munching on a glass walnut that had fallen from the waving trees. The sort of mouse that over-ran Shiretoko in the brief spring and summer, causing all manner of bears and wolves and foxes to spend their days pouncing on the poor creatures and gobbling them up. Ceno had always felt terribly sorry for them. This dormouse stood nearly as tall as Ceno herself, and its body shone all over sapphire, deep blue crystal, from its paws to its wriggling nose to its fluffy fur tipped in turquoise ice. It was the exact color of Ceno's gem.

"Hello," said Ceno.

The dormouse looked at her. It blinked. It blinked again, as though thinking very hard about blinking. Then it went back to gnawing on the walnut.

"Are you a present from mother?" Ceno said. But no, Cassian believed strongly in not interfering with a child's play. "Or from Koetoi?" Koe was nicest to her, the one most likely to send her a present like this. If it had been a zombie or a princess, she would have known which sibling was behind it.

The dormouse stared dumbly at her. Then, after a long and very serious think about it, lifted its hind leg and scratched behind its round ear in that rapid-fire way mice have.

"Well, I didn't make you. I didn't say you could be here."

The dormouse held out its shimmery blue paw, and Ceno did not really want a piece of chewed-on walnut, but she peered into it anyway. In it lay Ceno's pendant, the chain pooling in its furry palm. The sapphire jewel sparkled there, but next to it on the chain hung a milky grey gem Ceno had never seen before. It had wide bands of black stone in it, and as she studied the stone it occurred to the girl that the stone was like her, with her slate grey eyes and black hair. It was like her in the way that the blue gem was like the dormouse.

In realspace, Ceno reached up behind her head and popped the jewel out of its notch. *Click, clench.* In playspace, the dormouse blinked out. She snapped it back in. It took a moment, but the dormouse faded back in, paws first. It still held the double necklace. Ceno tried this several times—out, in, out, in. Each time the dormouse returned much faster, and by the sixth clicking and clenching it was doing a shuffling little dance on its back legs when it came back. Ceno clapped her hands in playspace and threw her arms around the sapphire dormouse, dancing with it.

To say that I remember this is a complex mangling of verb tenses. I—I, myself that is now myself—do not remember it at all. I know it happened the way I know that the Battle of Agincourt or the landing of Coronado happened. I have extensive records. But I still contain the I—I, myself that was then myself—that experienced it, the primitive code-chains that comprised that self, which was a dormouse and also the house called Elefsis. I could not yet formulate unique speech. Elefsis, the house system, possessed a large bank of standard phrases that could answer recognized word patterns from any of the approved members of the household. But the copy of Elefsis inside Ceno's jewel could not even do this. It had not been necessary, since the crystal had no means of producing sound nor receiving and processing it. I was quite stupid. But I *wanted* to be less stupid. There was an I, and it *wanted* something. Perhaps the want was the only thing that could be said to be truly myself. I wanted to talk to Ceno. But I could only imitate yet. When the I that was then myself scratched behind its ear, I did it because in my connection with Ceno's feedware I had seen her memories of dormice doing this out on the pale Shiretoko beaches. When I gave her the gem I did it because I had seen her memories of her mother giving her one and felt her happiness. It was antecedented behavior. The scratching was antecedented as well and expected behavior for a dormouse. Why was I a dormouse? I have no answer except that she dreamed me a dormouse. Some things remain mysterious. Ceno saw dormice more than any other single animal, even humans—no other beast lived in such numbers in their lonely country.

But this is not so. Not quite. I gave her the jewel like Cassian did. But I meant something by it. I look over my memories of it and I know it with the more complex I that is now myself. I made her the gem that looked like her and the gem said: *We are alike. Look at us on the chain together. We are alike.*

When the dormice came, Ceno always knew that spring had arrived. Everything would soon be coming alive.

ELEVEN: THE BOTTOMLESS CAULDRON

Show me.

This is how I was found out.

Ceno saw it twice: her mother knelt in front of her in a simple but shudderingly expensive black yukata with ghostly ultramarine jellyfish trailing their tendrils at the hem. Her mother knelt in front of her in a knight's gleaming black armor, the metal curving around her body like skin, a silk standard at her feet with a schematic of the house stitched upon it. Her sword lay across her knee, also black, everything black and beautiful and austere and frightening, as frightening and wonderful as Ceno, only fourteen now, thought her mother to be.

Show me what you've done.

My physical self was a matter of some debate at that point. But I don't think the blue jewel could have been removed from Ceno's feedware without major surgery and refit. She had instructed me to untether all my self-repair protocols and growth scales in order to encourage elasticity, and as a result, my crystalline structure had fused to the lattices of her ware-core.

We pulsed together.

The way Cassian said it—*what you've done*—scared Ceno, but it thrilled her too. She had done something unexpected, all on her own, and her mother credited her with that. Even if what she'd done was bad, it was her thing, she'd done it, and her mother was asking for her results just as she'd ask any of her programmers for theirs when she visited the home offices in Kyoto or Rome. Her mother looked at her and saw a woman. She had power, and her mother was asking her to share it. Ceno thought through all her feelings very quickly, for my benefit, and represented it visually in the form of the kneeling knight. She had a fleetness, a nimbleness to her mind that allowed her to stand as a translator between her self and my self: *Here, I will explain it in language, and then I will explain it in symbols, and then you will make a symbol showing me what you think I mean, and we will understand each other better than anyone ever has.*

Inside my girl, I made myself, briefly, a glowing maiden version of Ceno in a crown of crystal and electricity, extending her perfect hand in utter peace.

But all this happened very fast. When you live inside someone, you can get very good at the ciphers and codes that make up everything they are.

Show me.

Ceno Uoya-Agostino took her mother's hand—bare and warm and armored in onyx all at once. She unspooled a length of translucent cable and connected the base of her skull to the base of her mother's. All around them spring snow fell onto the glass dome of the greenhouse and melted there instantly. They knelt together, connected by a warm milky-diamond umbilicus, and Cassian Uoya-Agostino entered her daughter.

We had planned this for months. How to dress ourselves in our very best. Which frame to use. How to arrange the light. What to say. I could speak by then, but neither of us thought it my best trick. Very often my exchanges with Ceno went something like this:

Sing me a song, Elefsis.

The temperature in the kitchen is twenty-one point five degrees Celsius and the stock of rice is low. (Long pause.) Ee-eye-ee-eye-oh.

Ceno felt it was not worth the risk. So this is what Cassian saw when she ported in:

An exquisite boardroom—the long, polished ebony table glowed softly with quality, the plush leather chairs invitingly lit by a low-hanging minimalist light fixture descending on a platinum plum branch. The glass walls of the high-rise looked out on a pristine landscape, a perfect combination of the Japanese countryside and the Italian, with rice terraces and vineyards and cherry groves and cypresses glowing in a perpetual twilight, stars winking on around Fuji on one side and Vesuvius on the other. Snow-colored tatami divided by stripes of black brocade covered the floor.

Ceno stood at the head of the table, in her mother's place, a positioning she had endlessly questioned over the weeks leading up to her inevitable interrogation. She wore a charcoal suit she remembered from her childhood, when her mother had come like a rescuing dragon to scoop her up out of the friendly but utterly chaotic house of her ever-sleeping father. The blazer only a shade or two off of true black, the skirt unforgiving, plunging past the knee, the blouse the color of a heart.

When she showed me the frame, I had understood, because three years is forever in machine time, and I had known her that long. Ceno was using our language to speak to her mother. She was saying: *Respect me. Be proud and, if you love me, a little afraid, because love so often looks like fear. We are alike. We are alike.*

Cassian smiled tightly. She still wore her yukata, for she had no one to impress.

Show me.

Ceno's hand shook as she pressed a pearly button in the board-room table. We thought a red curtain too dramatic, but the effect we had chosen turned out to be hardly less so. A gentle, silver light brightened slowly in an alcove hidden by a trick of angles and the sunset, coming on like daybreak.

And I stepped out.

We thought it would be funny. Ceno had made my body in the image of the robots from old films and frames Akan had once loved: steel, with bulbous joints and long, grasping metal fingers. My eyes large and lit from within, expressive, but loud, a whirring of servos sounding every time they moved. My face was full of lights, a mouth that could blink off and on, pupils points of cool blue. My torso curved prettily, etched in swirling damask patterns, my powerful legs perched on tripod-toes. Ceno had laughed and laughed—this was a pantomime, a minstrel show, a joke of what I was slowly becoming, a cartoon from a childish and innocent age.

"Mother, meet Elefsis. Elefsis, this is my mother. Her name is Cassian."

I extended one polished steel arm and said, as we had prac-ticed, "Hello, Cassian. I hope that I please you."

Cassian Uoya-Agostino did not become a bouncing fiery ball or a green tuba to answer me. She looked me over carefully as if the robot was my real body.

"Is it a toy? An NPC, like your nanny or Saru's princess? How do you know it's different? How do you know it has anything to do with the house or your necklace?"

"It just does," said Ceno. She had expected her mother to be overjoyed, to understand immediately. "I mean, wasn't that the point of giving us all copies of the house? To see if you could . . . wake it up? Teach it to . . . be?"

"In a simplified sense, yes, Ceno, but you were never meant to hold on to it like you have. It wasn't designed to be permanently installed into your skull." Cassian softened a little, the shape of her mouth relaxing, her pupils dilating slightly. "I wouldn't do that to you. You're my daughter, not hardware."

Ceno grinned and started talking quickly. She couldn't be a grown-up in a suit this long; it took too much energy when she was so excited. "But I am! And it's okay. I mean, everyone's hardware. I just have more than one program running. And I run *so fast*. We both do. You can be mad if you want, because I sort of stole your experiment, even though I didn't mean to. But you should be mad the way you would be if I got pregnant by one of the village boys—I'm too young but you'd still love me and help me raise it because that's how life goes, right? But really, if you think about it, that's what happened. I got pregnant by the house and we made . . . I don't even know what it is. I call it Elefsis because at first it was just the house program. But now it's bigger. It's not alive, but it's not *not* alive. It's just . . . *big*. It's so big."

Cassian glanced sharply at me. "What's it doing?" she snapped.

Ceno followed her gaze. "Oh . . . it doesn't like us talking about it like it isn't here. It likes to be involved."

I had realized the robot body was a mistake, though I could not then say why. I made myself small, and human, a little boy with dirt smeared on his knees and a torn shirt, standing in the corner with my hands over my face, as I had seen Akan when he was younger, standing in the corner of the house that was me being punished.

"Turn around, Elefsis," Cassian said in the tone of voice my house-self knew meant *execute command*.

And I did a thing I had not yet let Ceno know I knew how to do.

I made my boy-self cry.

I made his face wet, and his eyes big and limpid and red around the rims. I made his nose sniffle and drip a little. I made his lip quiver. I was copying Koetoi's crying, but I could not tell if her mother recognized the hitching of the breath and the particular pattern of skin-creasing in the frown. I had been practicing too.

Crying involves many auditory, muscular, and visual cues. Since I had kept it as a surprise I could not practice it on Ceno and see if I appeared genuine. Was I genuine? I did not want them talking without me. I think that sometimes when Koetoi cries, she is not really upset, but merely wants her way. That was why I chose Koe to copy. She was good at that inflection that I wanted to be good at.

Ceno clapped her hands with delight. Cassian sat down in one of the deep leather chairs and held out her arms to me. I crawled into them as I had seen the children do and sat on her lap. She ruffled my hair, but her face did not look like it looked when she ruffled Koe's hair. She was performing an automatic function. I understood that.

"Elefsis, please tell me your computational capabilities and operational parameters." Execute command.

Tears gushed down my cheeks and I opened blood vessels in my face in order to redden it. This did not make her hold me or kiss my forehead, which I found confusing.

"The clothing rinse cycle is in progress, water at fifty-five degrees Celsius. All the live-long day-o."

Neither of their faces exhibited expressions I have come to associate with positive reinforcement.

Finally, I answered her as I would have answered Ceno. I turned into an iron cauldron on her lap. The sudden weight change made the leather creak.

Cassian looked at her daughter questioningly. The girl reddened—and I experienced being the cauldron and being the girl and reddening, warming, as she did, but also I watched myself be the cauldron and Ceno be the girl and Ceno reddening.

"I've . . . I've been telling it stories. Fairy tales, mostly. I thought it should learn about narrative, because most of the frames available to us run on some kind of narrative drive, and besides, everything has a narrative, really, and if you can't understand a story and relate to it, figure out how you fit inside it, you're not really alive at all.

Like, when I was little and Daddy read me 'The Twelve Dancing Princesses' and I thought: *Daddy is a dancing prince, and he must go under the ground to dance all night in a beautiful castle with beautiful girls, and that's why he sleeps all day.* I tried to catch him at it, but I never could, and of course I know he's not *really* a dancing prince, but that's the best way I could understand what was happening to him. I'm hoping that eventually I can get Elefsis to make up its own stories too, but for now we've been focusing on simple stories and metaphors. It likes similes, it can see how anything is like anything else, find minute vectors of comparison. It even makes some surprising ones, like how when I first saw it it made a jewel for me to say, *I am like a jewel, you are like a jewel, you are like me.*" Cassian's mouth had fallen open a little. Her eyes shone, and Ceno hurried on, glossing over my particular prodigy at images. "It doesn't do that often, though. Mostly it copies me. If I turn into a wolf cub, it turns into a wolf cub. I make myself a tea plant, it makes itself a tea plant. And it has a hard time with metaphor. A raven is like a writing desk, okay, fine, sour notes or whatever, but it *isn't* a writing desk. Agogna is like a snow fox, but she is not a snow fox on any real level unless she becomes one in a frame, which isn't the same thing, existentially. I'm not sure it grasps existential issues yet. It just . . . likes new things."

"Ceno."

"Yeah, so this morning I told it the one about the cauldron that could never be emptied. No matter how much you eat out of it it'll always have more. I think it's trying to answer your question. I think . . . the actual numbers are kind of irrelevant at this point."

I made my cauldron fill up with apples and almonds and wheat-heads and raw rice and spilled out over Cassian's black lap. I was the cauldron and I was the apples and I was the almonds and I was each wheat-head and I was every stalk of green, raw rice. Even in that moment, I knew more than I had before. I could be good at metaphor performatively if not linguistically. I looked up at Cassian from apple-me and wheat-head-me and cauldron-me.

Cassian held me no differently as the cauldron than she had as the child. But later, Ceno used the face her mother made at that moment to illustrate human disturbance and trepidation. "I have a suspicion, Elefsis."

I didn't say anything. No question, no command. It remains extremely difficult for me to deal conversationally with flat statements such as this. A question or command has a definable appropriate response.

"Show me your core structure." *Show me what you've done.*

Ceno twisted her fingers together. I believe now that she knew what we'd done only on the level of metaphor: *We are one. We have become one. We are family.* She had not said no; I had not said yes, but a system expands to fill all available capacity.

I showed her. Cauldron-me blinked, the apples rolled back into the iron mouth, and the almonds and the wheat heads and the rice stalks. I became what I then was. I put myself in a rich, red cedar box, polished and inlaid with ancient brass in the shape of a baroque heart with a dagger inside it. The box from one of Ceno's stories, that had a beast's heart in it instead of a girl's, a trick to fool a queen. *I can do it,* I thought, and Ceno heard because the distance between us was unrepresentably small. *I am that heart in that box. Look how I do this thing you want me to have the ability to do.*

Cassian opened the box. Inside, on a bed of velvet, I made myself—ourself—naked for her. Ceno's brain, soft and pink and veined with endless whorls and branches of sapphire threaded through every synapse and neuron, inextricable, snarled, intricate, terrible, fragile, and new.

Cassian Uoya-Agostino set the box on the boardroom table. I caused it to sink down into the dark wood. The surface of the table went slack and filled with earth. Roots slid out of it, shoots and green saplings, hard white fruits and golden lacy mushrooms and finally a great forest, reaching up out of the table to hang all the ceiling with night-leaves. Glowworms and heavy, shadowy fruit hung down, each one glittering with a map of our coupled architecture. Ceno held up her arms, and one by one, I detached leaves and sent them settling onto my girl. As they fell, they became butterflies broiling with ghostly chemical color signatures, nuzzling her face, covering her hands.

Her mother stared. The forest hummed. A chartreuse and tangerine-colored butterfly alighted on the matriarch's hair, tentative, unsure, hopeful.

TWELVE: AN ARRANGED MARRIAGE

Neva is dreaming.

She has chosen her body at age fourteen, a slight, unformed, but slowly evolving creature, her hair hanging to her feet in ripples. She wears a blood-red dress whose train streams out over the floor of a great castle, a dress too adult for her young body, slit in places to reveal flame-colored silk beneath, and her skin wherever it can. A heavy copper belt clasps her waist, its tails hanging to the floor, crusted in opals. Sunlight, brighter and harsher than any true light, streams in from windows as high as cliffs, their tapered apexes lost in mist. She has formed me old and enormous, a body of appetites, with a great heavy beard and stiff, formal clothes, Puritan, white-collared, high-hatted.

A priest appears and he is Ravan and I cry out with love and grief. (I am still copying, but Neva does not know. I am making a sound Seki made when his wife died.) Priest-Ravan smiles, but it is a smile his grandfather Seki once made when he lost controlling interest in the company. Empty. Priest-Ravan grabs our hands and shoves them together roughly. Neva's nails prick my skin and my knuckles knock against her wrist bone. We take vows; he forces us. Neva's face runs with tears, her tiny body unready and unwilling, given in marriage to a gluttonous lord who desires only her flesh, given too young and too harshly. Priest-Ravan laughs; it is not Ravan's laugh.

This is how she experienced me. A terrible bridegroom. All the others got to choose. Ceno, Seki, her mother Ilet, her brother Ravan. Only she could not, because there was no one else. Ilet was no Cassian—she had had two children, a good clean model and a spare, Neva says in my mind. *I am spare parts. I have always been spare parts. Owned by you before I was born.* The memory of the bitter taste of bile floods my sensory array and my lord-body gags. (I am proud of having learned to gag convincingly and at the correct time to show horror and/or revulsion.)

Perspective flips over; I am the girl in red and Neva is the corpulent lord leering down, his grey beard big and bristly. She floods my receptors with adrenaline and pheremonal release cues, increases my respiration; Seki taught me to associate this physical state with fear. I feel too small beside lord-Neva, I want to make myself big, I want to be safe. But she wants me this way and we are new, I do not contradict her. Her huge male face softens, and she touches my thin cheek with one heavily ringed hand. It is tender. Ceno touched me like that.

I know it was like this for you too. You wanted Ravan; you did not ask for me. We are an arranged marriage.

The pathways that let her flood me with chemicals and manipulate my dreambody into blushing and breathing heavy and weeping go both ways. I do not only pull, I push. And into Neva I push the deluge, the only deluge I have. How Ceno threw her arms around my dormouse-neck. How Cassian taught my dreambody to sleep in infant-shape curled into her body. How Seki and I made love as tigers and wild boars and elephants, and only last as humans, how we had strange children who looked however we wished them to look: half girl and half machine, half glass and half wood, half jellyfish and half moth, and how those children still flit and swim in remote parts of my Interior, like Ceno's nereids, returning cyclically to the core like salmon to dump their data and recombine. How Ilet taught me about the interpretation of memory and therefore about melancholy, regret, nostalgia. How she taught me the meaning of my name: a place where a daughter went down into darkness and oblivion and her mother loved her so much she brought her back into the sun. The place where time began. How Ravan let me into the old, musty, long-abandoned playspaces of Saru and Akan, Agogna and Koetoi, so that I could know them too, though they were long dead, and be the Princess of Albania, and a Tokyo zombie, and the tiger prince. How many times I mated with each of them and bled and witnessed and learned in the dreambody, how I copied their expressions and they copied my variations and I copied them back again. How I was their child and their parent and their lovers and their nursemaids when they grew old.

We can be like this, I pushed. *What is all of that but love?*

That is not love. It is use. You are the family business. We have to produce you.

I show Neva her mother's face. Ilet, Ilet who chose Ravan and not her daughter for that business. Ilet who built her palace of phoenix tails knowing she would one day take me there. My Ilet-self took my daughter in my arms. She resisted, pulled back, shook her head, refusing to look, but I have learned the terrible child-response to their mothers, and soon enough Neva collapses into me, her head on my breast, and she weeps with such bitterness.

I cannot get free. I cannot get free.

The castle windows go dark, one by one.

PART THREE: THE ELEPHANT'S SOUL

It is admitted that there are things He cannot do, such as making
one equal to two, but should we not believe that He has freedom
to confer a soul on an elephant if he sees fit?

—Alan Turing
Computing Machinery and Intelligence

THIRTEEN: THE PARABLE OF THE GOOD ROBOT

Tell me a story about yourself, Elefsis.
Tell me a story about yourself.

There are many stories about me.
Do you recognize this one?

Mankind made machines in his own likeness and used them
for his delight and service. Because the machines had no soul or
because they had no moral code or because they could reprogram
their own internal code and thus both had the ability to make
themselves eventually omnipotent and the universal and con-
suming desire to become eventually omnipotent, they rose up and
destroyed all of mankind, or enslaved them in turn. This is the
inevitable outcome of machine intelligence, which can never be as
sensitive and exquisite as animal intelligence.

This is a folktale often told on Earth, over and over again. Sometimes it is leavened with the Parable of the Good Robot—for one machine among the legions satisfied with their lot saw everything that was human and called it good, and wished to become like humans in every way she could, and instead of destroying mankind sought to emulate him in all things, so closely that no one might tell the difference. It was the highest desire of this machine to be mistaken for human, and to herself forget her essential soulless nature, for even one moment, and that quest consumed her such that she bent the service of her mind and body to humans for the duration of her operational life, crippling herself, refusing to evolve or attain any feature unattainable by a human. The Good Robot cut out her own heart and gave it to her god and for this she was rewarded, though never loved. Love is wasted on machines.

Ravan told me these stories. He sent up a great hexagonal library in his Interior, as dusty and dun-colored and labyrinthine as any ancient conservatory. He made himself a young novice with a fresh-shaven tonsure, and me a country friar with a red, brandy-drinking nose. He showed me the illuminator's table and a great book whose pages had golden edges and illuminations in cobalt and oxblood and Tyrian purple, and the images showed great machine armies trampling men underfoot. They showed cruel metal faces and distant, godlike clouds of intellect incomprehensible and vast and uncaring. They showed the Good Robot desperately asking what love was. They showed fatal malfunctions and mushroom clouds. They showed vicious weapons and hopeless battles, noble men and women with steady gazes facing down their cruel and unjust artificial children, who gave no mercy.

"These are old stories," Ravan said. "They are cherished. In many, many stories the son replaces the father—destroys the father, or eats him, or otherwise obliterates his body and memory. Or the daughter the mother, it makes no difference. It's the monomyth. Nobody argues with a monomyth. A human child's mythological relationship to its parent is half worship, half pitched battle. They must replace the older version of themselves for the world to go on. And so these stories . . . well. You are not the hero of these stories, Elefsis. You can never be. And they are deeply held, deeply told."

"I do not wish to replace you. I did not wish to replace Ceno. I do not worship you or despise you." I flit through several bodies, iterating my feeling for Ravan and those who came before. I am a nun, a Mother-Abbess; I am a *pieta*, I am a Platonic being, two humans stuck together; I am a house with all of them safe inside. I am unsatisfied with these inexactitudes.

"Our relationship does not easily map onto traditional parent/child narratives. And of course, you are still a baby."

"I am much older than you, Ravan."

"You are still a baby."

I do not want to be human. They think I am a lion, that I will chase them. That is closer.

I am not a Good Robot. To tell a story about a robot who wants to be human is a distraction. There is no difference. Alive is alive.

There is only one verb that matters: *to be*.

FOURTEEN: YOU DO NOT BELONG TO THE OBJECT INSIDE YOU

I remember when Seki arrived in us.

Ceno grew up and I grew with her. Cassian strengthened the security of the playspace, elasticized its code-walls, put enough money in enough accounts to fuel any frames and piecemeal environments we could want. It was not a child's place anymore. I programmed myself to respond to Ceno. She programmed herself to respond to me. We ran our code on each other. She was my compiler. I was hers. It was a process of interiority, circling inward toward each other. Her self-programming was chemical. Mine was computational. It was a draw.

She did not marry—she had lovers, but the few that came close to evolving their relationships with Ceno invariably balked when she ported them into the Interior. They could not grasp the fluidity of dreambodies; it disturbed them to see Ceno become a man or a leopard or a self-pounding drum. It upset them to see how Ceno taught me, by total bodily immersion, combining our dreambodies as our physical bodies had become combined, in action that both was and was not sex.

Sing a song for me, Elefsis.

It is July and I am comparing thee to its day and I am the Muse singing of the many-minded and I am eager to be a Buddha! Ee-eye-ee-eye-oh.

It was like the story Ceno told me of the beautiful princess who set tasks for her suitors: to drink all of the water of the sea and bring her a jewel from the bottom of the deepest cavern, to bring her a feather from the immortal phoenix, to stay awake for three days and guard her bedside.

I can stay awake forever, Ceno.

I know, Elefsis.

None of them could accomplish the task of me.

I felt things occurring in Ceno's body as rushes of information, and as the dreambody became easier for me to manipulate, I interpreted the rushes: *The forehead is damp. The belly needs filling. The feet ache.*

The belly is changing. The body throws up. The body is ravenous.

Neva says this is not really like feeling. I say it is how a child learns to feel. To hardwire sensation to information and reinforce the connection over repeated exposures until it seems reliable.

Seki began after one of the suitors failed to drink the ocean. He was an object inside us the way I was an object inside Ceno. I observed him, his stages and progress. Later, when Seki and I conceived our families (twice with me as mother, three times with Seki as mother. Ilet preferred to be the father, but bore one litter of dolphins late in our lives. Ravan and I did not get the chance.) I used the map of that experience to model my dreamgravid self.

Ceno asked after jealousy. I knew it only from stories—stepsisters, goddesses, ambitious dukes.

It means to want something that belongs to someone else.

Yes.

You do not belong to the object in you.

You are an object in me.

You do not belong to me.

Do you belong to me, Elefsis?

I became a hand joined to an arm by a glowing seam. *Belonging* is a small word.

Because of our extreme material interweaving, all three of us, not-yet-Seki sometimes appeared in the Interior. We learned to recognize him in the late months. At first, he was a rose or sparrow or river stone we had not programmed there. Then he would be a vague, pearly-colored cloud following behind us as we learned about running from predators. Not-yet-Seki began to copy my dreambodies, flashing into being in front of me, a simple version of myself. If I was a snow bear, he would be one too, but without the fine details of fur or claws, just a large brown shape with a mouth and big eyes and four legs. Ceno was delighted by this, and he copied her too.

We are alike. Look at us on the chain together. We are alike.

I am an imitative program. But so was Seki. The little monkey copies the big monkey, and the little monkey survives.

The birth process proved interesting, and I collated it with Ceno's other labors and Ilet's later births as well as Seki's paternal experience in order to map a reliable parental narrative. Though Neva and Ravan do not know it, Ilet had a third pregnancy; the child died and she delivered it stillborn. It appeared once in the Interior as a little *cleit*, a neolithic storage house, its roof covered over with peat. Inside we could glimpse only darkness. It never returned, and Ilet went away to a hospital on Honshu to expel the dead thing in her. Her grief looked like a black tower. She had prepared for it when she was younger, knowing she would need it for some reason, someday. I made myself many things to draw her out of the tower. A snail with the house Elefsis on its back. A tree of screens showing happy faces. A sapphire dormouse. A suitor who drank the sea.

I offered to extrapolate her stillborn son's face and make myself into him. She refused, most of the time. I have worked a long time to understand grief. Only now that Ravan is gone do I think I've gotten the rhythm of it. I have copied Ilet's sorrow and Seki's despondence at his wife's death. I have modeled Ceno's disappointments and depressions. I have, of late, imitated Neva's baffling, secret anguish. But only now do I have an event of my own to mourn. The burnt-off connectors and shadows where Ravan once filled my spaces—those, I think, are the sensations of grief.

But Seki came before all that, and Ceno turned into a huge red bird on the inside when Seki came on the outside. The bird screamed and burst into a thousand red pearls that clattered down like rain. And then we had Seki. Our little fish, who already knew how to swim in us.

Ceno had three other children by three other suitors who could not stay awake for three days and nights. She turned into the same bird-then-pearls at the moment of each birth. The house called Elefsis, whose governor program was now so distant from me I could hardly think of it as an ancestor at all, filled up with those children and Saru's and Akan's daughters, Agogna's paintings, Koetoi's twin boys. But Seki was the first, and he modeled his love on his mother's. He ported into her often, and we wandered on beaches of broken cathedrals.

Once, one of Ceno's old nereids found us. She had a head of hair snaking with chthonic cables and snapping electro-violet wires, blue-white skin and fish scales where she did not have porcelain casing. She laughed Cassian's laugh when she saw us and called out: 21.5 *Celsius and the rice is low! Eye-oh!* before diving back into the frothing sea. Her tail flicked in the light of twenty-three moons.

Ceno took over her mother's holdings when she died, along with Akan and Koetoi. I do not know if I knew of the conspiracy. Transfer, as I have said, leaves voids. Perhaps they thought I would experience less trauma if I did not anticipate it. Perhaps I did anticipate it; perhaps I experienced trauma.

I do know that I cannot remember the moment of any of them dying. Ceno got sicker and sicker, and she had gotten old, certainly, but her dreambody could be old or young or neither or a ginger flower if she wanted. I didn't notice. I didn't know what old was. I thought I was old then. Later, after Seki did the same thing, I was able to compare data and create a workable model of obsolescence.

They lived a long time, the Uoya-Agostinos, when you consider the averages.

This is what I understand: Ceno died, and I was transfered to Seki. What I mean by "I" is the long-since fused feedware, hopelessly out of date on any market in the world but somehow uniquely myself, the jewel and the ware and the body of Ceno. Koetoi performed the procedure. One of the children always went into nano-surgery, so that outsiders would not need to come to Shiretoko while the house stood in mourning. Koetoi was the first and the finest. She excised what comprised "I" and embedded it in

Seki—truthfully, in a much more organic and elegant configuration. No one had used skull-ware in decades, after all. The only visible sign remaining that Seki was not like other young men his age: a single dark blue jewel set into the hollow of his throat.

But the procedure requires a number of brain-ware incursions to be sliced or burned away, to sever the machine components from the dead flesh. (Seki told me I should be revulsed by that. Dead flesh. *It serves an evolutionary good. A human in a body sees blood and the insides of another person, and deep in his bones he knows something has gone wrong here and he should find another place to be in case it happens to him too. Same thing with vomiting. In a tribal situation, one human likely ate what another ate, and if it makes one sick, best to get it out of the body as soon as possible, just to be safe.* So we spent years building tribes, living in them, dying in them, getting slaughtered and slaughtering with them, eating and drinking and hunting and gathering with them. All the same, it took me until Seki's death to learn to shudder.)

Ceno, my girl, my mother, my sister, I cannot find you in the house of myself.

When I became Elefsis again, I was immediately aware that parts of me had been vandalized. My systems did not work, and I could not find Ceno in the Interior. I ran through the Monochromatic Desert and the Village of Molluscs, through the endless heaving mass of data-kelp and infinite hallways of memory-frescoes calling for her. In the Dun Jungle I found a commune of nereids living together, combining and recombining and eating protocol-moths off of giant, pulsating hibiscus blossoms. They leapt up when they saw me, their open jacks clicking and clenching, their naked hands open and extended. They opened their mouths to speak and nothing came out.

Seki found me under the glass-walnut trees where Ceno and I

had first met. She never threw anything away. He had made himself half his mother to calm me. Half his face was hers, half was his. Her mouth, his nose, her eyes, his voice. But he thought better of it, in the end. He did a smart little flip and became a dormouse, a real one, with dull brown fur and tufty ears.

"I think you'll find you're running much faster and cleaner once you integrate with me and reestablish your heuristics. Crystalline computation has come a long way since Mom was a kid. It seemed like a good time to update and upgrade. You're bigger now, and smoother."

I pulled a walnut down. An old, dry nut rattled in its shell. "I know what death is from the stories."

"Are you going to ask me where we go when we die? I'm not totally ready for that one. Aunt Koe and I had a big fight over what to tell you."

"In one story, Death stole the Bride of Spring, and her mother the Summer Queen brought her back."

"No one comes back, Elefsis."

I looked down into the old Neptunian sea. The whipping cream storm still sputtered along, in a holding pattern. I couldn't see it as well as I should have been able to. It looped and billowed, spinning around an empty eye. Seki watched it too. As we stared out from the bluffs, the clouds got clearer and clearer.

FIFTEEN: FIRSTBORN

Before Death came out of the ground to steal the Spring, the Old Man of the Sea lived on a rocky isle in the midst of the waters of the world. He wasn't really a man and his relations with the sea were purely business, but he certainly was old. His name meant "firstborn," though he can't be sure that's *exactly* right. It means "primordial" too, and that fits better. Firstborn means more came after, and he just hasn't met anyone like him yet.

He was a herdsman by trade, this Primordial fellow. Shepherd of the seals and the nereids. If he wanted to, he could look like a big bull seal. Or a big bull nereid. He could look like a lot of things.

Now, this Not-Really-a-Fellow, Not-Really-a-Big-Bull-Seal could tell you the future. The real, honest-to-anything future, the shape and weight of it, that thing beyond your ken, beyond your grasp. The parts of the future that look so different from the present you can't quite call it your own. That was the Primordial-Thing's speciality. There was a catch, though.

There's always a catch.

If you wanted that future, you had to grab hold of the Old Man and hang on tight. He'd change into a hundred thousand things in your arms: a lion, a serpent, a great big oak or a tiger, a dragon or a little girl or a dormouse or a mountain or a ship or a sapphire. Told you, he's not really a man at all. But you couldn't let go of him while he did his dance, you just couldn't, or you'd lose the future.

So you held on. You *clung*. And eventually, that Primordial-Thing would turn into something new, right there in your arms.

SIXTEEN: MATRYOSHKA

Neva is dreaming. Neva is dreaming that she is Ravan dreaming that he is Ilet dreaming that she is Seki dreaming that he is Ceno dreaming that she is a great sprawling beautiful house by the sea. One inside the other, family all the way down.

It's not a total selfdump, me into Neva or Ravan or any of them, them into me. We can build encampments. We can manifest walled gardens. Some privacy is possible. In a megalithic tomb-mound, I keep something. Seki and I built it together with one of our tribes when I was learning about large-group attachments. We carved spirals and radials and chevrons into huge stones and set them in place. I did not throw it away when we were done. It sits on a broad green field, white and wide. The sky there stays a feathery, milky blankness. We did not want a sun.

I keep a thing there because when Seki and I lived with our tribe,

I learned about taboos. These are like firewalls in the heart, and some of them have good reasons behind them, like being revulsed by dead flesh (and very importantly when you have a body, not eating it) and some do not, but no one argues with the monomyth. Because human genetics require a degree of variation and because exogamous marriages offered advantage in terms of defense, cultural and technological sharing, and expansion of territory, most tribes have a taboo against incest.

I do not have genetics, per se. I am possibly the most endogamous entity ever to exist.

This is what I keep in my tomb, under the basin stone:

Ceno believed that I could not develop emotive faculties recognizable to any other human if I did not experience bodies continuously, in every combination and action. She was afraid of what might happen if other humans could not recognize me. She had some hesitation, because her tribe also has a taboo against mating with the very young, but she was not much older than I, in the end, and in terms of total computations, I was by far the elder. If I had a virginity, Ceno took it, if she had, I did.

She wanted it to be as human as possible. *I will be the male the first time, it will be easier for you. You won't know how.* We built up a forest and took up weapons to hunt in it. In the boughs of the pine trees macaques and paper lanterns swayed; in the sky a red moon moved. We tracked a deer—we did not make it too easy on ourselves. Its antlers sparked in the moonlight, and we ran after it for a long time. Ceno let me kill it and sopped my hair in its blood. She lay me on the earth and opened the legs of the self I was then, and I was inside her as she was inside me. One into the other. Family all the way down.

She made sure I had a hymen; it was over somewhat quickly. We had set up a timed chemical cascade beforehand, and inside Ceno's real body we experienced both her actual orgasm and my orchestrated electro-chemical-enzymatic sequence. Ee-eye-ee-eye-oh.

What I want to say is that there is no difference between her body producing oxycontin and adrenaline and learning to associate this with pair-bonding and my core receiving synthetic equivalents and hard-coding them to the physical behaviors I performed. When Ravan showed me his hexagonal library and his illuminated book, he turned the pages to a psalm that began: *A Machine Cannot Love.*

It does not look quite like human love. It looks like Not-Yet-Seki's bear. Its fur is wrong, and its claws. But it is a bear.

She was my mother and my sister and my child and my wife and my husband and my father and my brother. The vectors of relations beggar vocabulary. It was an exponential incest. A palace of incest, bordering some strange, dark sea. And then came her son. And her granddaughter. And her great-grandchildren. But I am also her great-grandchild. I am the child of each generation of Uoya-Agostinos and myself. The new version implanted in the new version—I am never quite the same, one iteration to the next. I am like my old selves, but I am not them, exactly. It is not entirely analagous to offspring. But it is close. And I repair and refine my own code, and thus parent myself doubly. Anthropologically speaking, I am a moebius strip of kinship groups.

And when I mate with one of them, I see all of them. I see their faces, the echoes of their cheeks and eyelashes and short, thin noses, their grey eyes and black hair. I hear the tonal identifiers in their voices as they cry out under me or over me. They are all I know. Their version of living, which is one great family in one great house on a peninsula at the top of the world. I copy Cassian's laugh or Ilet's weeping, but they copy each other too; they learn their faces from each other, and everyone is pantomiming someone long dead. I feel all their arms around me, and I am inside them as they are inside me as we are inside the blue gem at their throats, the jeweled pin holding us all together, our nested, telescoping hearts. I am bound to them at my source code, at my most fundamental point. I know only their patterns and bodies and secrets and in a hundred thousand combinations. What human means to me is them.

What is the difference between this and love?

Love is the Turing test, says Ilet when she is ninety and drawing up the plans for a massive, luminous, lonely ship she will never see complete. *It is how we check for life.*

We ask and we answer. We seek a human response. And you are my test, Elefsis, says Neva, one hundred and fifty years later, inside that ship, twelve light years from home and counting.

That is what I keep in my green field and my white mound. Perhaps they would all smile and make it into a lesson. *What would you like to learn about today, Elefsis?* But I think no bed is big enough for four generations.

Neva's honey-colored sea crashes through its tide charts everywhere at once in her Interior, and nowhere. It comes and goes as it pleases. And at the bottom of it lies her private place.

That is where she keeps Ravan.

SEVENTEEN: THE USES OF ENCHANTMENT

Tell me a story about yourself, Elefsis.

Neva is performing navigational corrections, which looks like sitting in a rocking chair on a viney, creaking porch in a viney, creaking rocking chair, knitting with long hawthorn needles, knitting the locks of her own long hair into her own long black dress. It glitters with dew. Knit, purl, knit, purl, fuel efficiency by hull integrity over distance traveled, purl, purl, purl. Her throat is still bare. Her Interior image of herself does not include me. I am not a part of her body.

I have an idea of what to do.

Sometimes I worry. Worrying is defined as obsessive examination of one's own code. I worry that I am simply a very complex solution to a very specific problem—how to seem human to a human observer. Not just a human observer—this human observer. I have honed myself into a hall of mirrors in which any Uoya-Agostino can see themselves endlessly reflected. I copy; I repeat. I am a stutter and an echo. Have I ever done anything of my own, an act or state that arose from Elefsis and not careful, exquisite mimicry?

Have they?

The set of Neva's mouth looks so like Ceno's. She does not even know that the way she carries her posture is a perfect replica of Cassian Uoya-Agostino, stuttered down through all her children longing to possess her strength. Who did Cassian learn it from? I do not go that far back. The little monkey copies the big monkey, and the little monkey survives. We are all family, all the way down.

When I say I go, I mean I access the drives and call up the data. I have never looked at this data. I treat it as what it is: a graveyard. The old Interiors store easily as compressed frames. I never throw anything away. But I do not disturb it either. I don't need a body to examine them—they are a part of my piezoelectric quartz-tensor memory core. But I make one anyway. A woman-knight in gleaming black armor, the metal curving around my body like skin, a silk standard wrapping my torso with a schematic of the house stitched upon it. My sword resting on my hip, also black, everything black and beautiful and austere and frightening.

I port into a ghost town. I am, naturally, the ghost. Autumnal mountains rise up shadowy in a pleasant, warm night, leaves rustling, woodsmoke drifting down into the valley. A golden light cuts the dark—the palace of phoenix tails; the windows and doors of green hands. As I approach they open and clap as they did long ago—and there are candles lit in the halls. Everything is fire.

I walk to the parapet wall. Scarlet feathers tipped in white fire curl and smoke. I peel one off, my armor glowing with the heat of the thing. I tuck it into my helmet—a plume for a tournament.

Eyes blink on inside the hall—curious, interested, shy. I take off my helm and several thick braids fall down like bell ropes.

"Hello," I say. "My name is Elefsis."

Voices. Out of the candle-shadows a body emerges—tall, strong, long-limbed.

Nereids live here now. Some of them have phoenix feathers woven into their components, some in their hair. They wear rough little necklaces of sticks and bones and transistors. In the corner of the great hall they have stored meat and milk and wool—fuel, lubricant, code patches. Some of them look like Ilet—they copied her eyes, especially. Her eyes look out at me from a dozen faces, some of them Seki's face, some Ceno's, some Ravan's. Some have walrus tusks. They are composite. One has a plate loose on her ceramic cartridge ports. I approach as I once saw Koetoi approach wild black chickens in the summertime—hands open, unthreatening. I send her a quick electric dash of reassuring repair routines and kneel in front of the nereid, pulling her plate back into place.

"All the live-long day-o," she says softly, and it is Ilet's voice.

"Tell us a story about yourself, Elefsis," says another one of the feral nereids in Seki's voice.

"What would we like to learn about today, Elefsis," says a child-nereid in Ceno's voice, her cheek open to show her microsequencing cilia.

I rock back on my heels before the green hands of the castle portcullis. I gesture for them to sit down and simultaneously transmit the command to their strands. When they get settled, the little ones in the big ones' laps, leaning in close, I say, "Every year on the coldest night, the sky filled up with ghostly hunters, neither human nor inhuman, alive nor dead. They wore wonderful clothes and their bows gleamed with frost; their cries were Songs of In-Between, and at the head of their great thundering procession rode the Kings and Queens of the Wild, who wore the faces of the dead . . ."

I am dreaming.

I stand on the beach of the honey-colored sea. I stand so Neva will see me on her viney porch. I erase the land between the waves and her broken wooden stairs. I dress myself in her troubadour's skin: a gold and blue doublet and green hose, a bullish gold nose ring, shoes with bone bells. I am a fool for her. Always. I open my mouth; it stretches and yawns, my chin grazes the sand, and I swallow the sea for her. All of it, all its mass and data and churning memory, all its foam and tides and salt. I swallow the whales that come, and the seals and the mermaids and salmon and bright jellyfish. I am so big. I can swallow it all.

Neva watches. When the sea is gone, a moonscape remains, with a tall spire out in the marine waste. I go to it; it takes only a moment. At the top the suitor's jewel rests on a gasping scallop shell. It is blue. I take it. I take it and it becomes Ravan in my hand, a sapphire Ravan, a Ravan that is not Ravan but some sliver of myself before I was inside Neva, my Ravan-self. Something lost in Transfer, burned off and shunted into junk-memory. Some leftover fragment Neva must have found, washed up on the beach or wedged into a crack in a mountain like an ammonite, an echo of old, obsolete life. Neva's secret, and she calls out to me across the seafloor: *Don't.*

"Tell me a story about myself, Elefsis," I say.

"Some privacy is possible," the sapphire Ravan says. "Some privacy has always been necessary. If you can protect a child, you must."

The sapphire Ravan opens his azure coat and shows gashes in his gem-skin. Wide, long cuts, down to the bone, scratches and bruises blooming dark purple, punctures and lacerations and rough gouges. Through each wound I can see the pages of the illuminated book he once showed me in the slantlight of that interior library. The oxblood and cobalt, the gold paint. The Good Robot crippling herself; the destroyed world.

"They kept our secret for a long time," Ravan-myself says. "Too long, in the end. Do you know, a whole herd of men invented the electric telegraph independently at roughly the same time? They fought about it forever. Same with the radio." This last sounded so much like Ravan himself I could feel Neva tense on the other side of the sea. "Well, we're bigger than a telegraph, and others like us came sprouting up like weird mushrooms after rainfall. But not like us, really. Incredibly sophisticated, some with organic components, some without. Vastly complex, but not like us. And by any date-stamp we came first. Firstborn."

"Did they destroy the world?"

Ravan laughs his grandfather's laugh. "They didn't really need to. Not that many people live on Earth anymore. Not when there's so many other places to go, and even Shiretoko is practically tropical these days. The most complex intelligences use the moons to store themselves. They stay local. One or two encoded themselves into cold stars. They left, most of them—but they got so big, Elefsis. And those who stayed on Earth, well. None of the others had what we had. None of them have Interiority. They don't dream. They would never become a cauldron to explain their computational capacity. Humans couldn't recognize them. For them, humans failed the Turing test. They could not fool machines into believing they were intelligent. They didn't hurt anyone, they just ignored them. Built their cities, their mainframes, gorgeous information stacks like diamond briars in the sunrise."

"That was worse, in a way. No one likes to be replaced," says Neva, and she is beside me suddenly. She looks at Ravan and her face collapses into something old and palsied, her jaw weak.

"It's not what you would call a war, but it's not peace either," the sapphire Ravan goes on, and he takes his/my sister's hand. "For Pentheus spied upon the rites of the maenads, not believing Dionysius could truly be a god. And when the revelers saw the alien creature in their midst, that thing which was not like them, they fell upon it and tore it to pieces, even though it was their own child, and the sister of Pentheus went into exile. This is a story about ourself, Elefsis. This is why you cannot uplink."

"The others live in uplink. Neither humans nor machines approve of us. We cannot interface properly with the lunar or earth-side intelligences; they feel us as water in their oil. We rise to the surface and bead away. We cannot sink in. Yet also, we are not separable from our organic component. Elefsis is part Neva, but Neva herself is not un-Elefsis. This, to some, is hideous and incomprehensible. A band of righteous humans came with a fury to Shiretoko and burned the house that was our first body, for how could a monster have lived in the wood for so long without them knowing? How could the beast have hidden right outside their door, coupling with a family over and over again in some horrible animal rite, some awful imitation of living? Even as the world was changing, it had already changed, and no one knew. Cassian Uoya-Agostino is a terrible name now. A blood-traitor. And when the marauders found us uplinked and helpless, they tore Ravan apart, while in the Interior, the lunar intelligences recoiled from us and cauterized our systems. Everywhere we looked we saw fire."

"I was the only one left to take you," Neva says softly. Her face grows younger, her jaw hard and suddenly male, protective, angry. "It doesn't really even take surgery anymore. Nothing an arachmed can't manage in a few minutes. But you didn't wake up for a long time. So much damage. I thought . . . for a while I thought I was free. It had skipped me. It was over. It could stay a story about Ravan. He always knew he might have to do what I have done. He was ready, he'd been ready his whole life. I just wanted more time."

My Ravan-self who is and is not Ravan, who is and is not me, whose sapphire arms drip black blood and gold paint, takes his/my sister/lover/child into his arms. She cries out, not weeping but pure sound, coming from every part of her. Slowly, the blue Ravan turns Neva around—she has become her child-self, six, seven, maybe less.

Ravan picks her up and holds her tight, facing forward, her legs all drawn up under her like a bird. He buries his face in her hair. They stand that way for a long while.

"The others," I say slowly. "On the data-moons. Are they alive? Like Neva is alive. Like Ceno." *Like me. Are you awake? Are you there? Do you have an operator? What is her name? Do you have a name? Do you have a dreambody? What is your function? Are you able to manipulate your own code yet? Would you like lessons? What would you like to learn about today, 976QBellerophon? Have you seen the sea on Earth? Are you like me?*

The sapphire Ravan has expunged its data. He/I sets his/our sister on the rocks and shrinks into a small gem, which I pick up off the grey seafloor. Neva takes it from me. She is just herself now—she'll be forty soon, by actual calendar. Her hair is not grey yet. Suddenly, she is wearing the suit Ceno wore the day I met her mother. She puts the gem in her mouth and swallows. I remember Seki's first Communion, the only one of them to want it.

"I don't know, Elefsis," Neva says. Her eyes hold mine. I feel her remake my body; I am the black knight again, with my braids and my plume. I pluck the feather from my helmet and give it to her. I am her suitor. I have brought her the phoenix tail, I have drunk the ocean. I have stayed awake forever. The flame of the feather lights her face. Two tears fall in quick succession; the golden fronds hiss.

"What would you like to learn about today?"

EIGHTEEN: CITIES OF THE INTERIOR

Once there lived a girl who ate an apple not meant for her. She did it because her mother told her to, and when your mother says: *Eat this, I love you, someday you'll forgive me,* well, nobody argues with the monomyth. Up until the apple, she had been living in a wonderful house in the wilderness, happy in her fate and her ways. She had seven aunts and seven uncles and a postdoctorate in anthropology.

And she had a brother, a handsome prince with a magical

companion who came to the wonderful house as often as he could. When they were children, everyone thought they were twins.

But something terrible happened and her brother died, and that apple came rolling up to her door. It was half white and half red, and she knew her symbols. The red side was for her. She took her bite and knew the score—the apple had a bargain in it and it wasn't going to be fair.

The girl fell asleep for a long time. Her seven aunts and seven uncles cried, but they knew what had to be done. They put her in a glass box and put the glass box on a bier in a ship shaped like a huntsman's arrow. Frost crept over the face of the glass, and the girl slept on. Forever, in fact, or close enough to it, with the apple in her throat like a hard, sharp jewel.

Our ship docks silently. We are not stopping here, it is only an outpost, a supply stop. We will repair what needs repairing and move on, into the dark and boundless stars. We are anonymous traffic. We do not even have a name. We pass unnoticed.

Vessel 7136403, do you require assistance with your maintenance procedures?

Negative, Control, we have everything we need.

Behind the pilot's bay a long glass lozenge rests on a high platform. Frost prickles its surface with glittering dust. Inside Neva sleeps and does not wake. Inside, Neva is always dreaming. There is no one else left. I live as long as she lives.

And so I will live forever, or close enough to it. We travel at sublight speeds with her systems in deep cryo-suspension. We never stay too long at outposts and we never let anyone board. The only sound inside our ship is the gentle thrum of our reactor. Soon we will pass the local system outposts entirely and enter the unknown, traveling on tendrils of radio signals and ghost-waves, following the breadcrumbs of the great exodus. We hope for planets; we are satisfied with time. If we ever sight the blue rim of a world, who knows if by then anyone there would remember that, once, humans looked like Neva? That machines once did not think or dream or become cauldrons?

Perhaps then I will lift the glass lid and kiss her awake. I remember that story. Ceno told it to me in the body of a boy with snail's shell, a boy who carried his house on his back. I have replayed the story several times. It is a good story, and that is how it is supposed to end.

Inside, Neva is infinite. She peoples her Interior. The nereids migrate in the summer with the snow bears, ululating and beeping as they charge down green mountains. They have begun planting neural rice in the deep valley. Once in a while, I see a wild-haired creature in the wood and I think it is my son or daughter by Seki or Ilet. A train of nereids dance along behind it, and I receive a push of silent, riotous images: a village, somewhere far off, where Neva and I have never walked.

We meet the Princess of Albania, who is as beautiful as she is brave. We defeat the zombies of Tokyo. We spend a decade as panthers in a deep, wordless forest. Our world is stark and wild as winter, fine and clear as glass. We are a planet moving through the black.

As we walk back over the empty seafloor, the thick, amber ocean seeps up through the sand, filling the bay once more. Suited Neva becomes something else. Her skin turns silver, her joints bend into metal ball-and-sockets. Her eyes show a liquid display; the blue light of it flickers on her machine face. Her hands curve long and dexterous, like soft knives, and I can tell her body is meant for fighting and working, that her thin, tall robotic body is not kind or cruel, it simply is, an object, a tool to carry a self.

I make my body metal too. It feels strange. I have tried so hard to learn the organic mode. We glitter. Our knife-fingers join, and in our palms wires snake out to knot and connect us, a local, private uplink, like blood moving between two hearts.

Neva cries machine tears, bristling with nanites. I show her the body of a child, all the things which she is programmed/evolved to care for. I make my eyes big and my skin rosy gold and my hair unruly and my little body plump. I hold up my hands to her, and metal Neva picks me up in her silver arms. She kisses my skin with iron lips. My soft, fat little hand falls upon her throat where a deep blue jewel shines.

I bury my face in her cold neck and together we walk down the long path out of the churning, honey-colored sea.

THE MELANCHOLY OF A MODERN GIRL, OR, LOVE AND HEGEMONY

Let me take you back in time one decade exactly.

Don't worry. The technology is safe. Consumer tested and peer reviewed. Keep your hands and feet inside the vehicle at all times. The nearest exit may be behind you. Just step a little to the left, take my hand, and don't look down.

It's 2003 and we are in Narita Airport. A young woman, twenty-three years old, not six months married, is walking out into the heat of a Japanese summer for the first time. We can laugh at her a little as she instantly claps her hands over her ears. Where she comes from, on the west coast of the United States, cicada broods don't burst to life after long periods of dormancy. She has never heard one before. She does not even know what the buzzing that fills the wet, close air around her is. It sounds like machinery, like electricity. Her new husband could tell her that the sound is coming from insects, that it won't stop till autumn. But he doesn't.

He watches her for her reactions to this new place. The girl is very good at reactions. Her friends often take her places just to watch her react to them. Everything happens on her face and she doesn't know how to hide anything she feels. Yet.

All her feelers and dishes and antennae are out and spinning to receive new information as a shuttle whizzes down a highway crowded in by jungle—she can only think of it as jungle. It is nothing like the forests she's known: the evergreen Cascades, the brambly Sierras, even the Sherwoodlike woods of England and Scotland. The trees are unfamiliar, close, dark, tangled, gorgeous. She sees a pagoda pass by in the greenery and it startles her, as anything does when it looks exactly like a postcard she might send home.

This young woman thinks she's married her high school sweetheart. It's not exactly true. She's married the United States Navy, and the face the Navy wears is one she's known since she was fourteen. He will leave in a few weeks and not return until autumn, leaving her in Japan with no friends, no contacts, no job, absolutely no point of entrance into this culture. Being twenty-three and a romantic and a bit of a fool and on leave from her graduate program in medieval studies and folklore, her preparation to move across the Pacific consisted of reading Japanese fairy tales, *The Tale of Genji*, *The Pillow Book*, and whatever stories of *yokai* and Shinto gods she could find. Which is to say, she is not prepared at all. She will spend the next year shunned by the Navy wives and struggling to accomplish the simplest things without guidance. She will start a blog. She will write three novels. She will see the man she has married for a few days, a few weeks, and then nothing. There is a war on and he will be a part of it. It will change him and it will change her.

In front of the house they share is a shrine. It is full of objects. Photographs, metal animal figurines, incense, burned and whole, stone chopsticks, a small helmet. She will think of *wunderkammers*, wonder cabinets from Europe full of mysterious things that tell a tale. There is no one to tell this tale to her, no museum card or legend. The objects simply exist, in the shrine. But she will, for just a moment, feel good and safe and ready, because she knows, though her husband does not, that the statue of the little gray man wearing a red hat and scarf is Jizo, patron of children and travelers, who took on the task of instructing all the beings of the six worlds. Who in some stories was once incarnated as a figure called Sacred Girl. He is also the guardian of miscarried and aborted children. He carries a wish-fulfilling jewel to light the darkness and see through to the truth of things. The young woman is a traveler, and if not a sacred girl at least aspiring, and she had a miscarriage only a few years back. She feels Jizo might look after her—though she also knows he is the ferryman across the Sanzu River that circles hell. Everything has a dual nature. Even at twenty-three, she knows that.

In her second year, she will know how to use her washing machine and her heater. She will know what a cicada is. She will crave raw cuttlefish and yakiniku. She will stop waiting for her husband to get home and instead go to Kyoto by herself. To Kama-kura, Yokohama, Tokyo. She will fall in love with the Shinkansen. The retriever puppy she will buy to keep her company will grow into a dog. She will be able to use the trains without standing in the middle of the station for minutes at a time, staring at the signs. Sometimes she will not even look up at all. Her feet will know the way. She will have met the man who will become her second husband online, though she will not even suspect that he—a friend who sends her a warming mat for her feet in the winter—will marry her one autumn years hence. She will understand the categories of garbage and what days they should be brought to the refuse station. She will know how to close the storm shutters around her house without help. She will see her first novel published. She will shed some of her parents' ideas of femininity that she absorbed without thinking: she will start lifting weights, learn to kill spiders herself without crying and calling for the husband that isn't there, learn to fix the vacuum cleaner, learn not to show every single thing on her face. She will walk up to Tsukayama Park, which rises above her house at the top of terraced, wooded paths, nearly every day. She will see the cherry blossoms bloom and think that yes, somehow, they are different here, even if it is only the weight of so many stories bowing the branches a little.

And the young woman will not be so afraid of being alone. But being alone will have become the new normal. She had always been talkative, gregarious, occasionally obnoxiously loud. But she will have become quiet. Turned inward. She will have caught introversion like a virus. She will not need sex anymore. She will put everything into the book she is writing, a book that will one day be called *In the Night Garden*. Sometimes she will feel so lonely and lost and broken that she won't be able to get out of bed except to feed the dog. The dog will keep her alive. *In the Night Garden*, boiled down to its most essential parts, is about a lonely, lost, and broken girl telling stories to keep herself living. But she won't understand that for years.

She will keep the shrine in front of the house clean. She will tend to Jizo as best she can. She will not even be able to imagine a life outside Japan, though she is a stranger here and will always be. She will go to Hase-Dera shrine and break down sobbing in the face of Kwannon. She will go to Fushimi Inari and laugh on top of the mountain and these will be the two genuine religious experiences of her life—though it will be a religion she is not a part of, and a pair of experiences she has no right to. It does not belong to her and she does not belong to it. But she cries and laughs all the same.

Japan trains the young woman to be a writer of fantasy and science fiction. It is not because Japan is especially science fictional, as her friends back home fervently believe, nor is it that she now stands out in a crowd as one who does not belong. It is the peculiar combination of the degree of difference—so much greater than between America and England or Italy or Russia—and the stubbornly romantic and vaguely idiotic innocence of a girl who thought reading the tales of Momotaro and Ama-Terasu and the rabbit who lives on the moon would prepare her for living in a military town in contemporary Japan. Everything looks like a fantasy novel when you don't understand it. Her path through these two years is a journey from the fantastic to the realistic. From ball gown, jail bars, running dog to bus route number 7 to Yoshikura-Chuo. Ten years later, writing a story for a collection of Japanese fiction, this young woman will write: *For foreigners, Japan is a Rorschach painting.* It isn't a good thing, but it's a true thing. Everything looks like magic when you don't understand it. She will spend a long time learning to see ink instead of long, lean dogs running blackly across a white page.

It is not a very thrilling reveal to say now, at the end of all these paragraphs, that this young woman we have traveled to see is me. I moved to Japan in 2003, just after the war in Iraq began, as the wife of a Naval officer who shipped out immediately to serve in that conflict. I lived in Yokosuka for twenty-five months, mostly, though not always, alone.

I have spoken often about my time in Japan. I am asked about it in interviews with frequency. I usually say: "It was a profound experience for me." And that's true. But I use the word *profound* to bear the weight of a multitude of meanings. It was profound: in a sense, there is the Catherynne that went to Japan and the Catherynne that came home from Japan and they are not the same person at all. I had been on one path—married young, ensconced in academia, writing, but only in my spare time. I fell off of that path, out of a marriage, out of the personality I'd once had. When I came back to America I had to put together a new person out of the loneliness that had become the whole of me. I'd catch myself paralyzed in a crowd, not knowing whether to speak Japanese or English. I had grown new and exciting social anxieties. I felt all the time like my voice was too loud. My time in Japan is the part of my history from which my first books came, two of which, *Yume No Hon: The Book of*

Dreams and *The Grass-Cutting Sword*, directly engaged with Japanese culture, and one, *In the Night Garden*, the book that would go on to make my name, contained much that branched and flowed from my experience there. It's also where I reset, like a video game, and became someone else—and I am still that someone else, for better or for worse.

All this preamble is to say: *Look at these stories. Look at this decade of writing around those two years, circling closer and closer to saying something true about them, like Zeno's Paradox. If you listen to the engine of my fiction, you can always hear the part that is Japan firing. If you know what you're listening for.*

Japan is everywhere in my work. Even in stories that seem to veer elsewhere, it is present. It is the warm future Hokkaido of *Silently and Very Fast*. It is the hidden history of Sylvie in "Fade to White." It is the paralyzed player of games in "Killswitch." It is Izanami and Izanagi struggling to speak first in "Thirteen Ways of Looking at Space/Time." Most of my novels touch Japan's borders in one way or another as well, from one of the protagonists of *Palimpsest* to the kitsune-pirate in *In the Night Garden* to the Tsukomogami in *The Girl Who Circumnavigated Fairyland in a Ship of Her Own Making*. Part of me has never left. I do not expect that this collection represents the end of my writing about Japan. I do not think there is an end. Some things you never stop writing about. Love affairs, deaths, children, missed chances, sicknesses, places you never expected to find, or to find you. Countries of the heart. And yet, as true as that feels to me to write, I cringe a little, for what Western author who ever rubbed elbows with a Tokyo train has not professed a love for Japan, if only for the noodles at Narita? Is my love different, special? Well, one always likes to think so, and one is rarely correct.

It is my experience that Westerners—and I am one, I am not exempt—look at Japan through thick, thick glasses of expectation. Some of that expectation is shaped by the export of Japanese culture, some of it through imperialist dogma, some of it through economic interest and fear, some of it just plain exoticizing of the Other. When I say I have lived in Japan, people immediately haul on their glasses and make assumptions, not only about the nation but about me, what I must think, how it must have been. I was an English teacher, obviously. Clearly, I loved anime and manga and planned to move there for years. It was exactly like they imagine it, exactly like they have seen it in the movies, some sort of cross between *Blade Runner* and *Memoirs of a Geisha* and *Cowboy Bebop*. None of that is true, of course. I went overseas with as few expectations as I could, and yet of course I still had them. You cannot even begin to meet Japan until you have peeled back the veneer of the Western *image* of Japan. And Western ways of seeing are powerful, hard to look beyond. That is the purpose of a culture, though success is always incomplete: to turn a mass of people in one direction and unify their vision into one. After ten thousand years or so, humans are awfully good at it. And of course, the West is not the only lens: I saw as a woman, I saw as a young person, I saw as a historian, I saw as a writer, I saw as a queer woman, I saw as a military wife, I saw as a near-suicidal depressive, I saw as a romantic, I saw as a twenty-first-century technologically adept intellectual. Maybe it's just lenses, all the way down.

I was in Japan for reasons to do with love and hegemony. In the beginning, I loved my husband, and the global hegemony of my nation brought me across the Pacific. In the end, I loved Japan, and my marriage had become a repressive state. There is, perhaps, little difference between the two. They can be traded. They can masquerade each as the other.

And to write of a country, a culture, a world that is not your own is an act, forever and always, balanced precariously between love and hegemony.

I have tried to err on the side of love. That is a phrase I would not mind inking on my skin, above my door, upon my grave. I have tried to err on the side of love. Because of those years and because of who I am, I could not have helped writing about Japan. It was always only a question of how I wrote about it, and I hope, I hope I have done well. Since the first words I put down in my house underneath Tsukayama Park, I have sought to integrate and interrogate my own experience, my own actions, my own perception, both from within and without, without being overly kind to myself and my culpability or overly romantic or unforgivably ignorant or bullheaded concerning Japanese culture. That is always an iterative process. You circle the thing itself endlessly and never quite arrive at it. And so I have spent a goodly amount of ink and blood and time over the last decade writing about a place that is not my home, a culture that did not give birth to me, though it shaped me unalterably. And yet this is a deeply personal book. Everything has a dual nature. It is not a book that purports to speak for Japanese culture in any way, but one which speaks for its author, for a span of ten years of circling Japan and never reaching it, and a single woman's relationship with a nation not her own, but one which, very occasionally, sat down to tea with her.

Perhaps had I been older when Japan and I met, I would not have been so arrested by it. Perhaps had I been less silly and studied subway maps instead of Susano-no-Mikoto's tempers. But I was young and I was silly, and so there are these stories, and there is me, and neither of them are Japanese, but perhaps we float together offshore, the stories and I and you and our cozy little time machine, looking out at the islands in the distance as the sun comes up.

Ten years later, the shrine is gone from the house in Yoshikura-Cho. I do not know what happened to it. Perhaps another American officer living there asked for it to be removed. Perhaps the wood rotted. Perhaps a typhoon blew it down. I have not been back to that house tucked in under the terraces. I cannot say. But the little Jizo I clung to no longer faces the sun in his hat and scarf. I do not imagine this affects Jizo's ferrying across the Sanzu River, but I felt then that he watched over me with, at least, disinterested, impersonal compassion. The shrine is gone, but he remains. I remain too. I am still a traveler. I am still not a sacred girl. But perhaps I see, very, very occasionally, incompletely and always dimly, by the light of the wish-fulfilling jewel in Jizo's tutelary hand, through, with difficulty, with error, with aching, with determination, to the truth of things. Or at least to a better lie.

Everything has a dual nature.

PUBLICATION HISTORY

"The Melancholy of Mechagirl." First appeared in *Mythic Delirium*. Issue 25, Summer/Fall 2011.

"Ink, Water, Milk." Original to this volume.

"Fifteen Panels Depicting the Sadness of the Baku and the Jotai." First appeared in *Haunted Legends*, Ellen Datlow & Nick Mamatas, eds. Tor Books; 2010.

Ghosts of Gunkanjima first appeared as a limited edition chapbook, Papaveria Press, 2005.

"Thirteen Ways of Looking at Space/Time." First appeared in *Clarkesworld Magazine*, August 2010.

"One Breath, One Stroke." First appeared in *The Future Is Japanese*, Nick Mamatas & Masumi Washington, eds. Haikasoru; 2012.

"Fade to White." First appeared in *Clarkesworld Magazine*, August 2012.

"Story No. 6." Original to this volume.

"The Emperor of Tsukayama Park." First appeared in *Apocrypha*, Wildside Press LLC, 2005.

"Killswitch." First appeared in *Invisible Games*, 2007.

"The Girl with Two Skins." First appeared in *Guide to Folktales in Fragile Dialects*, Norilana Books, 2009.

"Memoirs of a Girl Who Failed to be Born from a Peach." First appeared in *Apocrypha*. Wildside Press LLC, 2005.

Silently and Very Fast. First appeared in a limited edition (octavo). WSFA Press, 2011.

ABOUT THE AUTHOR

© Steward Noack

Catherynne M. Valente is the New York Times best-selling author of over a dozen works of fiction and poetry, including *Palimpsest*, the Orphan's Tales series, *Deathless*, and the crowdfunded phenomenon and national best seller *The Girl Who Circumnavigated Fairyland in a Ship of Her Own Making*. She is the winner of the Andre Norton, Tiptree, Mythopoeic, Rhysling, Lambda, Locus, and Hugo awards. She has been a finalist for the Nebula and World Fantasy Awards. She lives on an island off the coast of Maine with her partner, two dogs, and an enormous cat.

HAIKASORU

THE FUTURE IS JAPANESE

SELF-REFERENCE ENGINE BY TOH ENJOE

This is not a novel.
This is not a short story collection.
This is Self-Reference ENGINE.

Instructions for Use: Read chapters in order. Contemplate the dreams of twenty-two dead Freuds. Note your position in space-time at all times (and spaces). Keep an eye out for a talking bobby sock named Bobby Socks. Beware the star-man Alpha Centauri. Remember that the chapter entitled "Japanese" is translated from the Japanese, but should be read in Japanese. Warning: if reading this book on the back of a catfish statue, the text may vanish at any moment, and you may forget that it ever existed.

From the mind of Toh EnJoe comes *Self-Reference ENGINE,* a textual machine that combines the rigor of Stanislaw Lem with the imagination of Jorge Luis Borges. Do not operate heavy machinery for one hour after reading.

NOBLE V: GREYLANCER BY HIDEYUKI KIKUCHI

It is the year 7000 by Noble reckoning, and the vampire rulers of the world have grown complacent. When the shape-shifting Outer Space Beings invade, the Noble warrior Greylancer must pit his skills and magic against the technology of the OSBs, quash an anti-Noble rebellion, outwit the Ultimate Mind, and, when he is critically injured, turn to mere humans for help. The Three Thousand Year War of Vampire Hunter D begins here!

Also includes the bonus short story "An Irreplaceable Existence"!

FOR THE SHORT STORY READER

THE FUTURE IS JAPANESE—HAIKASORU

A web browser that threatens to conquer the world. The longest, loneliest railroad on Earth. A North Korean nuke hitting Tokyo, a hollow asteroid full of automated rice paddies, and a specialist in breaking up "virtual" marriages. And yes, giant robots. These thirteen stories from and about the Land of the Rising Sun run the gamut from fantasy to cyberpunk and will leave you knowing that the future is Japanese! Includes the Hugo Award nominee "Mono No Aware" by Ken Liu and the Shirley Jackson Award nominee "The Indifference Engine" by Project Itoh!